To D[...]

Step into the adventure !

THE
ALCHEMIST'S
PORTRAIT

BY SIMON ROSE

[signature: Simon Rose]

VANCOUVER   LONDON

For Julie, Samuel and Georgia

Published in Canada by Tradewind Books Ltd.
www.tradewindbooks.com

Distribution in the UK by Turnaround

Distribution in Canada by Fitzhenry & Whiteside

9 8 7 6 5 4 3 2

Printed in China.

Manufactured by Kings Time Canada (Subsidiary of Nordica
International Ltd.)
Manufactured in Panyu, Guangzhou, China in Sept.09
Job# 07/34/09A

Text copyright © 2003 by Simon Rose
Cover illustration © 2003 by George Juhasz
Book design & pre-press by U&I Type Services Ltd.

Cataloguing-in-Publication Data for this book is available from the
British Library.

National Library of Canada Cataloguing in Publication Data

Rose, Simon, 1961-
   The alchemist's portrait / by Simon Rose

   ISBN 1-896580-29-7

   1. Magic – Juvenile fiction. 1. Title.
PS8585.O7335A82 2003   jC813'.6   C2003-910558-X
PZ7R718AI 2003

The Publisher thanks the Canada Council and the British Columbia Arts
Council for their support.

 Canada Council **Conseil des Arts**
for the Arts **du Canada**   BRITISH COLUMBIA
ARTS COUNCIL

The publisher also acknowledges the financial support of the Government
of Canada through the Book Publishing Industry Development Program
(BPIDP) and the Association for the Export of Canadian Books (AECB) for
our publishing activities.

CONTENTS

PROLOGUE

Peter rushed into the studio and slammed the door behind him. A moment later the door was blown off its hinges, and he was thrown against the far wall where his portrait hung.

"Do you realise with whom you are dealing, boy?" Nicolaas van der Leyden bellowed as he stormed into the studio. "I know more about the realm of magic than you could ever learn!"

"I cannot allow you to use my father's work for your own evil ends!" Peter replied defiantly.

"Your father was a fool!" snarled his uncle. "Now tell me where the magic paint is, or you will suffer the same fate!"

"But he destroyed it all!" protested Peter.

"I should never have let you live!" growled van der Leyden, and with a wave of his hand, he imprisoned Peter inside his portrait.

CHAPTER ONE

THE VOICE FROM NOWHERE

"And here we have another work from the same century."

No wonder everyone calls him Boring Goring, thought Matthew as his art teacher's voice droned on and on. Mr. Goring had a way of making even the most interesting subject dull.

Matthew loved art, and this exhibition of seventeenth-century Dutch paintings was a highlight of the year for him. Some of the paintings on display were from private collections, and had never been seen in public. Yet, thanks to Mr. Goring, this had to be Matthew's most boring visit to the museum ever.

"Not exactly *The Laughing Cavalier,* is he?" commented Matthew's best friend Alex, smirking as he gestured to the painting on the gallery wall beside them. "Looks like he's just as bored as we are."

Matthew had to agree. The painting was surrounded by an ornately carved wooden frame, and depicted a boy from the waist up. He was no more than thirteen or fourteen, and wore a wide-brimmed black hat. He had long sandy hair, which tumbled over a lace collar. The sleeves of his jacket had gold and blue swirling patterns, with white lace around the cuffs. He had a thin, unsmiling mouth, and his expression was blank. The eyes in particular were cold and lifeless.

"Too much of old Goring, if you ask me," whispered Alex, nudging his friend with his elbow. His freckled face broke into a wide grin.

"Bet he was smiling before our group came in!" Matthew quipped.

"Matthew! Alex!" boomed Mr. Goring. "What is all the commotion about? Perhaps you wouldn't mind sharing it with the rest of us."

Matthew and Alex spun around to face their teacher, who stood frowning at them.

"Well? I'm waiting," he prodded.

"I... that is, we..." stammered Alex.

"What he means," interrupted Matthew, "is that this painting is pretty interesting."

2

"Ah yes," mused Mr. Goring, as he adjusted his half-moon glasses, moving closer to the portrait in front of them. "A most interesting piece, indeed. And it has quite a history, I might add."

Matthew skimmed frantically through the museum guidebook, searching for a description of the portrait.

"And just what exactly is so fascinating about it, Matthew?" Mr. Goring asked, turning to face the boys. "I'm sure everyone else is dying to know."

"Well," began Matthew, "it says in the guidebook that this is actually a portrait of the artist's nephew. It's kind of a mystery why he painted him with such a sad face."

The rest of the class gazed at the painting before them, and nodded their heads.

"It's similar to *The Laughing Cavalier*," continued Matthew, "but the boy in this portrait is certainly not laughing, is he?"

At this, all of Matthew's classmates started to snigger.

"All right, all right. Settle down," said Mr. Goring. "Actually, this portrait has been unofficially dubbed *The Gloomy Cavalier*."

"Told you," whispered Alex. "Too much Boring Goring."

Matthew jabbed him in the ribs with his elbow.

"You were saying, Matthew?" questioned Mr. Goring, keeping a stern eye on him.

"Um, that's it really," Matthew answered sheepishly.

"I would suggest reading the guidebook more closely," advised Mr. Goring, "before you try to give the rest of us a lecture in art, Matthew."

Mr. Goring then turned his attention to the class. "For the benefit of the rest of you, this painting is attributed to the Dutch artist Nicolaas van der Leyden of Amsterdam. It is supposed to be a portrait of the artist's nephew, Peter Glimmer, and was completed around 1660. There is a rumour that van der Leyden also painted a self-portrait, but none of his other works has survived. Van der Leyden himself mysteriously disappeared."

Mr. Goring strode off in the direction of another painting, and the students shuffled along after him. Matthew remained behind, curious about the portrait in front of him.

While he skimmed through his guidebook looking for more information about *The Gloomy Cavalier,* he heard a voice call out his name.

"Matthew!"

"What now, Alex?" Matthew sighed, looking up from the book.

But Alex wasn't there. Matthew quickly scanned the gallery, and easily spotted Alex's unruly mop of red hair at the other end of the room.

"Matthew!" the same voice repeated.

Matthew's head snapped back to stare at the portrait of Peter Glimmer. The voice was coming from the painting! He thought for a moment that he saw Peter Glimmer's eyes move and a smile form on his mouth.

My eyes must be playing tricks on me, he thought.

The next instant, he heard a more familiar voice behind him. "Are you coming or not?" asked Alex.

"Does this picture look any different to you?" Matthew asked Alex, regaining his composure.

"He looks as miserable as ever," answered Alex, with a shrug.

"I could have sworn I saw him smile, just for a second," began Matthew. He was about to add that he had also heard a voice, but thought better of it. Alex would think he was crazy.

5

"You've been in here too long," said Alex. "This dusty old museum's made your brain fuzzy. And it's bothering my allergies too!"

Just then, Alex let out a thunderous sneeze, loud enough to rattle the paintings in their frames. A museum guard, half-dozing in a chair, sat up with a start.

"Good one," said Alex proudly, wiping his nose on his sleeve. "I came back to tell you that Old Goring is letting us take a snack break. Let's go to the cafeteria."

The two boys turned and walked out of the Portrait Gallery.

The entrance to the cafeteria was located just off the museum's Egyptian Room. Alex went straight to the food line, while Matthew grabbed a seat at an empty table and opened his guidebook. He couldn't get the portrait of Peter Glimmer out of his mind. Just as he began to read about it, two of his classmates sat down at his table.

"Hey Matthew!" said Josh, taking the chair next to him.

"What are you reading?" Ethan said. "Do you think Goring's going to give us a test?"

"Um, no," said Matthew, putting the guidebook away. "I was just looking, that's all."

He found himself listening to Josh's description of all the cool stuff he got for his birthday. Then Alex joined them at the table with his cousin Kyle.

"Back me up on this, Matthew!" Alex demanded.

Alex and Kyle were always arguing about sports statistics. Matthew's thoughts drifted as the familiar debate went on.

Did I imagine that smile on his face? he thought. *Could I have imagined the voice, too?*

Matthew had to find out more. By now, his classmates weren't taking any notice of him, so he quietly got up and slipped out of the cafeteria.

He retraced his steps back to the Portrait Gallery. First he passed a room containing several dinosaur skeletons. Next was a room full of Greek and Roman sculptures, with a statue of a four-armed Indian goddess in the corner. He soon arrived at a wide circular area in the centre of the museum, where all the corridors intersected.

Sunlight gleamed through a dome in the roof, illuminating a mosaic map of the world set into the floor beneath it. Marble statues were everywhere. A life-sized Viking longship, complete with a dragon figurehead, stood at the entrance to the Medieval Room. The ship was filled with helmeted mannequins wearing fierce expressions. Matthew got his bearings and walked through the Medieval Room, hurrying past swords, axes and lances displayed in glass cases. Suits of armour lined one wall, next to a knight on an armoured horse.

He finally reached the now deserted Portrait Gallery. Standing once more in front of Peter Glimmer, Matthew took time to examine the unusual frame. Some of the animals portrayed in the carvings were mythological creatures he recognised, such as unicorns, centaurs and gryphons. Others were completely unfamiliar to him. In the background of the painting itself, he saw a wooden table. A wineglass lay tipped over on it, next to a bowl of fruit and a vase of blue flowers. Beyond, pale sunlight filtered in through an open window. Matthew stared hard at the face of this boy from so long ago, trying not to blink. The boy's eyes were lifeless, and there was no hint of a smile.

"Some people call him *The Gloomy Cavalier,* you know," said a voice beside him. "Weird frame, too."

Matthew looked over to see a young woman with friendly eyes. She was tall and slim, her hair cut even shorter than Matthew's. Her ears were covered with earrings. She was dressed in jeans and a plain white

T-shirt, to which was pinned a nametag that read *Tess Philips, Restorations.*

"Yes," replied Matthew. "Our teacher mentioned that."

"So you know a little about it?" Tess asked him.

"Yes, a little," said Matthew.

"Well, it's all stories, of course. Legends almost," said Tess, "but pretty fascinating all the same. They say that both Peter's father and Nicolaas van der Leyden, Peter's uncle, were alchemists."

"You mean they tried to turn things into gold?" asked Matthew.

"Perhaps," answered Tess. "Some people even say that van der Leyden dabbled in magic."

Magic! Matthew thought. He *knew* there was something odd about the picture in front of them.

"Just rumours, of course," Tess continued. "It's on public display for the first time in centuries. And soon we might have two van der Leydens in the gallery."

"Two?" said Matthew, even more intrigued.

"Oh yes," said Tess. "We're restoring the self-portrait at the moment."

"So there really is a self-portrait," said Matthew. "It's being restored here in the museum?"

"It is," confirmed Tess. "Say, would you be interested in seeing some of the restoration work?"

Just then, a cross voice barked from behind them, "Miss Philips!"

Matthew spun around to see a smartly dressed man in a black suit. Grey hair swept straight back from his forehead and he wore a small goatee on his chin. Matthew's attention was drawn to a nasty scar above the man's left eyebrow. The nametag on his lapel read *Albert Runsiman, Curator - Special Exhibits.*

"Oh hello, Mr. Runsiman," said Tess with a polite smile. "This is... Sorry, I've forgotten your name."

"Matthew."

"Right, of course. Mr. Runsiman, this is Matthew," said Tess. "Matthew's very interested in art. I was just telling him some of the stories about the mysterious Nicolaas van der Leyden."

"Perhaps," said Mr. Runsiman, his grey eyes shooting Tess a frosty look, "you'd be better off doing what you're paid for, Miss Philips, instead of filling this young man's head with nonsense."

Just then the curator's cell phone rang. When he put it to his ear, Matthew couldn't help but notice the green gemstone on his gold ring. Mr. Runsiman turned and left through a door marked *Staff Only,* indicating to Tess that she should follow him.

"It was nice talking with you, Matthew. But I have to get back to work," Tess said, disappearing through the same door.

Alone in the silent gallery, Matthew once again stood face to face with the portrait of an unhappy Peter Glimmer. This time the eyes did not move, and the mouth did not change expression. Giving up all hope of learning more, Matthew turned around to head back to the cafeteria. But before he could take a single step, he felt a sharp tug on his collar, and the gallery vanished.

CHAPTER TWO

THE ALCHEMIST'S NEPHEW

Matthew found himself in a small, cramped room. He looked around and realised with alarm that he recognised his surroundings. On a sturdy wooden table, beside an overturned wineglass, sat a bowl of fruit and a vase containing brilliant blue flowers. The shutters on the far wall were open, and Matthew dashed over to what he thought was a window. It turned out that it wasn't a window at all. Instead of a view to the outside, the shutters enclosed a painting of tall ships in a harbour at sunset. Matthew gently touched the canvas. It was still wet.

Where on earth am I? he thought, trying not to panic.

"Matthew."

Matthew felt as if someone had dropped an ice cube down his back. Forcing himself to turn around, he came face to face with a young boy with vivid blue eyes, whose shoulder-length hair tumbled over his lace collar.

Matthew was paralysed with fear.

"Don't come any closer," he choked. "Where am I?"

"But, surely you know?" said the boy, puzzled.

"Who are you?" demanded Matthew, dreading the answer.

"I am Peter Glimmer, Matthew," declared the boy. "I am a prisoner in my own portrait."

With a sweep of his arm, the painting of the harbour, the window shutters, and the surrounding walls rippled, as if they were liquid. The colours mingled, swirling together briefly before returning to their original state.

That's no painting of ships in a harbour. The entire room is a painting! Matthew thought. *I'm inside the portrait of Peter Glimmer!* Through what he supposed must be the portrait's frame, he caught sight of the gallery he had been standing in only moments before.

"Stay away from me," said Matthew. He felt like he was losing his mind.

13

"No one can see you in here, Matthew," Peter said softly, reaching toward him, the air rippling as he did.

"What do you want?" demanded Matthew, pulling away.

"Your help," Peter replied and stood still. "There is very little time. My uncle is ready to put his plan into operation, and it will spell disaster for the entire world."

"What are you talking about?" said Matthew, knitting his brow.

"Beware of my uncle's power. My father opposed him and paid for it with his life. I tried to stop my uncle, too, and this portrait prison was the result."

"Hang on," said Matthew, raising his hand for Peter to stop. "Your uncle? Do you mean Nicolaas van der Leyden?"

"My uncle's spell cast me into this painting," replied Peter. "He thinks that I am dead. But I have been observing him edge closer and closer to his goal."

"Observing him?" said Matthew, shaking his head again. "But he's been dead for over three hundred years. *You've* been dead for over three hundred years! What's going on?"

"Neither of us is dead, Matthew," insisted Peter. "My uncle is still very much alive, and you have already met him. I know this must be confusing for you, but the circumstances are dire. I cannot force you to help me. You must choose to do so freely. Please consider what I have said and return when you are ready to hear more."

"I don't understand," said Matthew, perplexed.

"When you come back, I will explain further," Peter replied.

With that, he waved his hand and Matthew was back in the museum gallery, staring once more into the grim face of Peter Glimmer.

This is way too weird, he thought.

Matthew sprinted out of the Portrait Gallery, almost colliding with a group of people standing at the entrance. He raced out through the Medieval Room, side-stepping visitors who were examining the mosaic. He didn't stop until he had reached the cafeteria entrance, nearly out of breath.

Mr. Goring was standing there with the rest of the class, and Matthew had never been so pleased to see him.

"Matthew! Where on earth have you been?" said Mr. Goring, angrily.

I wish I knew, Matthew thought to himself. "Sorry," he said aloud, breathing heavily. "I got lost."

"Got lost? What do you mean lost?" snapped Mr. Goring through clenched teeth. His neck was beginning to turn red.

"Excuse me, Mr. Goring," interrupted the bus driver. "I'm parked in front of the main entrance, and the security guards won't let me wait there much longer."

"Very well, very well," muttered Mr. Goring. "Come along, everyone. Time to go. Hurry now."

"So?" Alex persisted, as he and Matthew waited in line to get on the bus. It was beginning to rain, so they covered their heads with their jackets.

"Where were you? Old Goring nearly had a fit when he noticed you weren't with us."

"I'll tell you later," said Matthew, wishing Alex would just drop the subject. He needed time to think.

"Fine! Suit yourself!" huffed Alex, as he boarded the bus and rushed to the back to sit with Kyle. Matthew could hear them arguing loudly again as he took a seat near the front.

It was raining heavily by the time Matthew got off. Alex ignored him when he waved goodbye.

Matthew raced home, hurrying to get out of the rain. Once inside, he took off his coat and tossed it onto a chair. Then he went into the kitchen for a snack.

"How was the museum?" asked his mother, looking up from chopping vegetables.

"Definitely not boring," answered Matthew, grabbing a cookie from the jar on the counter.

"Dad's running a little behind," she continued. "He's picking Sally up from gymnastics. Dinner will be late."

"Okay!" said Matthew, as he bounded upstairs to his room two steps at a time.

The bookcase in the upstairs hall was crammed with volumes on history and art. Matthew was determined to learn more about the mysterious Nicolaas van der Leyden. He pulled out several books and took them to his room. Skimming through them at his desk, however, he found very little information. Even the five-hundred-page *Encyclopaedia of Art* revealed no more about van der Leyden than he already knew from the museum guidebook. He checked the Internet, but found nothing new there either.

Matthew was disappointed when he joined his family for dinner that evening. He distracted himself by entertaining his sister, Sally, with the story of Alex and his sneeze. He certainly didn't mention the voice he had heard in the Portrait Gallery, or his encounter with

Peter Glimmer inside the painting. He didn't want to worry his parents. They wouldn't understand. He himself didn't really understand what had happened.

After dinner, Matthew went back to his room. He tried watching television for a while, but couldn't get the events of the day out of his mind.

Did I really meet Peter Glimmer this afternoon? he thought. *And how could I have already met Nicolaas van der Leyden? Maybe Alex is right. Maybe my brain is getting fuzzy.*

Matthew wondered if anyone else had ever experienced anything like this. He flicked off the television and climbed into bed. Eventually he drifted off to sleep, his head still spinning.

CHAPTER THREE

THE MUSEUM REVISITED

Sunlight glinted through the blinds in Matthew's room. Rolling over, he pulled the pillow over his head, but the buzz of the alarm clock forced him to acknowledge the start of his day. He switched off the alarm and sat up, stretching and yawning as he swung his legs over the side of the bed. Yawning again, he noticed the time. Eight o'clock! He was going to be late. He leapt to his feet, and was about to fling open the closet doors when he realised that it was Saturday.

I could have slept in, he thought with a groan, before he remembered what he had to accomplish. He had to learn more about Nicolaas van der Leyden.

Of course! thought Matthew. *The woman from the museum! Tess something-or-other.*

He hurriedly got washed and dressed, and rushed downstairs. He was about to race out the front door when his mother called him from the kitchen.

"Matthew," she said. "Where are you off to?"

"The museum," he replied. "I have to go back there this morning."

"Not without breakfast you don't!" insisted his mother.

Matthew sat down at the table and absent-mindedly poured himself a huge bowl of cereal. Adding milk right up to the brim, he was so engrossed in his thoughts that he scarcely noticed his mother sitting across from him.

"Hey, Matthew," she said. "The grocery store called. They're running out of cereal."

"Huh?" mumbled Matthew with his mouth full.

"Honestly, Matthew!" she exclaimed. "Anyone would think you hadn't eaten for weeks!"

"Sorry," Matthew apologised, continuing to shovel cereal into his mouth.

"So, what's up?" she asked. "Did you forget something at the museum yesterday?"

"I met someone who repairs the damaged paintings there," explained Matthew. "She offered to let me look at some of her restoration work. I forgot all about it, until I got up this morning."

"Forgot to put your shirt on the right way, too," his mother pointed out with a chuckle.

"I was in a hurry," Matthew answered. He pulled his T-shirt back over his head and twisted it around. "I have to get going."

"Where to?" asked his sister as she walked into the kitchen.

"Nowhere," he said, nonchalantly.

The last thing I need is her tagging along, he thought. He made a beeline for the door before his mother tried to persuade him to take Sally along.

"What time will you be home?" asked his mother, but Matthew had already pulled the door shut.

There was a brisk breeze in the late November morning air as Matthew hurried downtown to the museum. From the pavement, Matthew stared at the imposing façade of the building, which took up an entire city block. Thick columns were evenly spaced between the windows, all along the front. A sweeping stone staircase led up to a pair of enormous wood-panelled doors at the museum's main entrance.

Matthew took a deep breath. *Here goes nothing,* he thought. Then he ran up the steps and pushed open one of the museum's heavy doors.

"Whoa, young fella," said the guard, who had just unlocked the front entrance. It was the same guard who had been awakened by Alex's sneeze the day before. "In a hurry, are we?" he chortled.

"Sorry," Matthew said as he rushed past.

Just inside the entrance, Matthew saw a sign that read *Administration Room.*

Maybe the restoration area is through here, he thought as he headed in that direction. He stopped in his tracks when he saw a sign on one of the doors that read *Albert Runsiman, Curator — Special Exhibits.* Matthew definitely didn't want to run into him.

"Hello," said Tess from behind him. "Matthew, isn't it?" she asked, smiling.

"Hi," said Matthew. "I thought I'd take you up on your invitation to show me the restoration area."

"Oh, right. I did say that, didn't I?" replied Tess. "I'm the only one here today. So I guess it'll be all right for me to show you around. Let me get a coffee before we start. I'll walk you down to the Restoration Room, and you can wait for me there."

Matthew had to hustle to keep up as Tess led the way. They cut through the gallery filled with dinosaur skeletons, and arrived at the Restoration Room.

"Here we are," said Tess, turning the door handle. "Have a look around while I go and grab that coffee. I'll be right back."

"Okay," said Matthew as he entered the dimly lit room.

The workshop was in complete disarray. Paintings, statues and fragments of pottery were everywhere. Some of the paintings were on easels. Others were on large, wide tables next to dirty coffee mugs. Jars of paint and cans of paint thinner were scattered around the room. He could smell epoxy resin and varnish. On one table was a mug with the name TESS written on it; on the floor underneath it he could see a book. Curious, he bent down to see what it was called. In the low light, he could just make out its title, *The Supernatural Revealed.* He stood up and looked around the room. In the far corner was another door. A leather jacket hung on a coat rack next to it.

Matthew wondered if one of the pictures being worked on was the other van der Leyden portrait. Then he spotted something on an easel in the corner, covered by a white sheet.

That must be it, he thought.

He made his way over to the covered painting and turned on a nearby lamp. Holding his breath, he gently lifted the sheet and hung it over the back of the easel. *Let's see what you look like,* he thought, as he stood back.

In the lamplight, Matthew could see the portrait of an older man with long grey hair and a wide-brimmed black hat. His jacket had the same type of coloured sleeves and lace cuffs as the one that Peter Glimmer wore in his portrait. To Matthew's frustration, the face was damaged, making it impossible to discern the man's features. In the top right corner a burn hole was being repaired. It was easy to tell that extensive restoration had already been done. Much of the paint looked like it had been freshly applied. There was a crease in the centre of the canvas from top to bottom, and the entire right half of the picture looked odd. It seemed to Matthew that there had once been something painted there, although it was impossible to say what.

Before he could study the picture further, he heard the door opening. Frantically, he replaced the white sheet just as Tess walked in.

"If you're interested in restoration work, you've come to the right place," she said. "This is where damaged paintings and artefacts are brought to be fixed."

As Tess sat down at the nearest table, she pushed aside a book called *Mysteries of the Unexplained.*

"It looks like a busy place," said Matthew.

"There are five people working here during the week," explained Tess. "But it's usually just me here on Saturdays."

She took a sip from her coffee. "This painting's from the eighteenth century," said Tess, pointing to a pretty young woman in a flowing red dress. "I'm not sure who she was, but it needed some serious work."

Matthew watched as Tess gently brushed the canvas. Her fingers were covered with just as many rings as her ears.

"Do you remember that I was looking at the portrait of Nicolaas van der Leyden's nephew when I met you yesterday?" he said.

"Ah," said Tess, nodding. *"The Gloomy Cavalier."*

"Yeah," said Matthew. "The guidebook says that only two of van der Leyden's works survive. Did you say that the other one was being restored?"

"Right. I did say that," replied Tess. "It's over there in the corner. Mr. Runsiman's the only one who

25

is allowed to work on it. I guess it would be okay for me to show it to you. It was in pretty bad shape. It's amazing that it survived at all. It was almost lost in a fire with all van der Leyden's other works."

"Is it really in such bad shape?" asked Matthew innocently, not wanting to reveal that he'd already seen it.

"Take a look yourself," she said.

Tess stood up and gestured for Matthew to come closer.

She lifted up the sheet, draping it carefully over the top of the easel. "People think that this is Nicolaas van der Leyden himself," she explained.

"Did there used to be something on the right-hand side of the canvas?" Matthew asked.

"Yeah," said Tess. "No one knows for sure. There's a story that it was once a double portrait. The blank side of the canvas was folded under the other side for centuries. It was discovered only recently. Scholars think there might have been a picture of Johan Glimmer, Peter's father, on the other side. He and van der Leyden were brothers-in-law."

"Are all the stories about van der Leyden true?" Matthew asked.

"Well, let me tell you," said Tess. "It's all pretty spooky stuff."

"Really?" said Matthew, trying to stay cool. "I've read a bit about the Dutch masters, but I'd love to know more about Nicolaas van der Leyden."

"Especially about him being a magician, I'll bet," said Tess with a wink.

CHAPTER FOUR

TALL TALES FROM TESS

Matthew's heart began to race.

"Are you okay?" asked Tess. "You look pale."

"Yes, I'm fine," said Matthew, his knees weakening.

"Are you sure?" Tess insisted.

"It's probably the fumes," he replied, sitting down on a nearby chair.

"It could be," agreed Tess. "Mr. Runsiman is a perfectionist. He even manufactures his own paint, right here in the museum. He has his own laboratory behind that locked door, where he works late into the night."

Tess pointed to a door at the far side of the room. "That's where the fumes are coming from. I'll turn on the exhaust fan."

"I'll be okay," said Matthew, keeping an eye on van der Leyden's portrait. Tess turned on the exhaust fan, and the room felt fresher.

"Ugh," Tess winced, drinking the dregs from her coffee cup as she replaced the sheet on the portrait. "The coffee from the staff room is terrible. Let's go to the cafeteria. I'll buy you a drink."

Tess grabbed her leather jacket from the coat rack, and pulled it over her shoulders as they walked towards the Restoration Room's rear door. The door swung open, and Matthew noticed that it didn't have a handle.

Matthew found himself in a small alcove filled with boxes and crates. Following Tess through a pair of thick red drapes, he emerged, to his surprise, in the museum's Egyptian Room. The passageway had brought them out behind an enormous, multi-coloured mummy case, which was at least eight feet tall. As they stepped out from behind the heavy drapes, a young woman shrieked in surprise.

"Gets folks every time, my little short cut," said Tess, with a laugh. "Let's hurry, before the cafeteria gets too busy."

Tess chose a table just inside the cafeteria. "I'll be right back," she said.

While he waited, Matthew started a mental check-list of the things he wanted to ask Tess.

"I got some cookies too," Tess said, returning with a tray of snacks.

"Thanks," said Matthew.

"So, what do you know about *The Gloomy Cavalier*?" asked Tess, as she emptied two sugar packets into her coffee.

"Very little," replied Matthew. "My teacher mentioned that the painting had an interesting history, and that van der Leyden had disappeared mysteriously. Then you told me about the alchemy and stuff."

"What do you know about alchemists, Matthew?"

"Just the stuff about trying to turn lead into gold," he replied.

"That's part of it," said Tess. "Alchemy started in ancient Egypt, but turned into the rudiments of science in the Middle Ages. The alchemists often dedicated their entire lives to the discovery of what they called the Philosopher's Stone."

"I think I read something about that," said Matthew.

"The Philosopher's Stone was supposed to enable alchemists to transform base metals, like iron and lead, into gold," Tess continued. "It was also supposed to enable people to live forever. No alchemist ever found the Philosopher's Stone as far as we know, but their discoveries laid the foundation for modern science. For example, during his experiments, one alchemist discovered how to make porcelain. Another accidentally created gunpowder. Some learned about acids and different types of gases."

"And that's the sort of thing van der Leyden did?" asked Matthew.

"Yes," said Tess, "but he was also an artist. In fact, Nicolaas van der Leyden and Johan Glimmer, Peter's father, were both well-known artists in their day. Johan Glimmer's paintings are scattered around the world in various museums and private collections."

Matthew waited as Tess took another sip from her coffee.

"And painting wasn't the limit of their talents," she went on. "Back in the seventeenth century, there weren't many doctors. Some people, like Glimmer and van der Leyden, did a kind of medical research. They were curious about the human body, and wanted to know how it worked. They hoped they could discover treatments for diseases. Johan Glimmer spent years searching for a cure for the disease that killed his wife when their son was still a baby. But cadavers for research were hard to come by."

"So what did the early doctors do?" Matthew asked.

"Well," Tess continued, "the prisons were often the best source. After executions, the prison authorities either didn't object to the bodies of criminals being removed for scientific research, or they turned a blind eye to the whole thing. There are also stories that bodies were stolen from graveyards in the dead of night. There were also reports that sometimes they didn't even wait until people were dead."

Matthew swallowed hard. He put the cookie to one side. Suddenly, he didn't feel like eating.

"You mean...?"

"That's right," Tess went on in a grim voice. "Some early doctors kidnapped people. In a place like Amsterdam, for example, where there were so many people coming and going, it would have been easy. There would have been people no one would ever miss. Creepy, eh?"

"Very. You mentioned that van der Leyden was a magician. Do you believe in magic?" asked Matthew.

"Well, there's a lot we can't explain, Matthew," replied Tess, with a frown. "Especially about van der Leyden's self-portrait, if you ask me."

"Like what?" asked Matthew.

"One night, I came back to the museum rather late to look for my wallet, which I had left behind," said Tess, lowering her voice. "I had the feeling that there was someone else there. When I looked around, the room was empty. But then van der Leyden's eyes in the painting seemed to be staring at me. It was really spooky."

Matthew felt a shiver run down his spine.

"I sometimes wonder if the painting's haunted," Tess continued, "but don't mention it to Mr. Runsiman."

"Why?" Matthew wanted to know.

"Mr. Runsiman seems obsessed with that painting," said Tess, rolling her eyes.

"How do you mean, obsessed?"

"Mr. Runsiman's a great boss — most of the time. But lately, he's become very anxious. He always works on the restoration at night, when no one else is there."

"When will it be done?" said Matthew.

"Not sure," said Tess, munching on the last cookie. "Not for a while yet. It's a miracle it's still in one piece. Did you know that there's another mystery associated with Peter Glimmer and his family? Peter, his father and van der Leyden all disappeared without explanation."

"All of them?" asked Matthew. "What happened?"

"Well," Tess began. "Johan Glimmer vanished when Peter was small, and no trace of him was ever found. Peter was brought up by his uncle. Then a few years later Peter and van der Leyden disappeared too."

"What happened?" Matthew asked again.

"No one knows," said Tess. "It's all the stuff of legend now. There was a fire in 1666, which some say destroyed all of van der Leyden's paintings. One thing is certain, whatever else happened on the night of the fire, neither Peter, nor his uncle, were ever seen again."

"But, not all the paintings were destroyed," said Matthew. "There are two of them in this museum."

"Yes, that's the strange thing," said Tess, her brow furrowing. "Just two paintings survived. Portraits of the alchemist and his nephew. Odd, don't you think?"

It sure is, thought Matthew as he nodded.

He was glad he'd made the trip back to the museum. Now he wanted to find out if Tess knew as much about the painting of Peter Glimmer as she did about the portrait of Nicolaas van der Leyden.

"Oops," said Tess, glancing at her watch, half-hidden by the multitude of bracelets that extended halfway up her arm. "I'd better be getting back to work."

"Do you know anything about Peter Glimmer's portrait?" asked Matthew, as Tess got up to leave.

"Sorry, Matthew. I have to run," Tess apologized, gulping the last of her coffee. "I'm only working until two o'clock today. Here's my business card. Give me a call."

Then she was gone.

Now it was Matthew's turn to look at his watch. Time certainly had flown. It was nearly noon, and Alex was due to come over to his house for a sleepover. He got up from the table, his mind reeling from all he had heard. He was positive that what had happened in the Portrait Gallery hadn't been his imagination. Peter Glimmer had been as real as Matthew himself, even if Peter *had* been dead for over three hundred years.

CHAPTER FIVE

MATTHEW'S MISSION

"Are you nuts?"

Matthew knew that Alex wouldn't believe him.

"You're psycho!" Alex said.

"I'm telling you, Alex," asserted Matthew in hushed tones, "there's something really weird going on."

"Are you talking about when you asked me if the picture of that gloomy kid looked any different?" asked Alex.

"That's right," said Matthew. "I was sure I heard someone call my name. I thought it was you and..."

"Hey, remember my monster sneeze?" asked Alex, proudly.

"Who could forget," said Matthew, irritated. "Anyway, when I heard that voice, I didn't understand what was going on. Then, when I was inside the portrait, I thought I was going crazy. But Tess..."

"Who's Tess?" said Alex, looking confused.

"The woman who works at the museum," said Matthew. "Alex, pay attention!"

"Sorry," replied Alex. "Carry on."

"Tess told me all about van der Leyden," Matthew went on, "including some bizarre stuff about him and Peter Glimmer. It made me think that I didn't imagine it after all. She showed me a back door into the Restoration Room too, and a pretty neat secret passage."

"Secret passage?" said Alex, raising his eyebrows.

"Yeah," continued Matthew. "You and I are going to go back to the museum later this afternoon, to hide until after closing time. Then we can sneak into the Portrait Gallery. My parents are going to be out this evening. It'll give us plenty of time. I'll have to leave Sally here all alone."

"We?" said Alex.

"Alex, I can't do this on my own," pleaded Matthew.

"You want us to break into the museum?" Alex looked unsure. "Suppose we get caught?"

"It's not really breaking in. Not exactly," Matthew reassured him. "Just hanging around a little after hours. Besides, I doubt if the guards they have would notice a *real* thief walking out with a ten-foot mummy case under his arm."

"I don't know, Matthew," said Alex, shaking his head.

"Look," explained Matthew, "Tess felt the portrait of Nicolaas van der Leyden was alive or something. She said she was sure that sometimes it was watching her at night. Like it was haunted."

Alex's eyes lit up.

"Haunted!" he exclaimed.

"Yeah, haunted," sighed Matthew.

"Cool," said Alex. "What time does the museum close?"

"So you'll come?" said Matthew, excitedly.

"You bet I'll come," said Alex. "Wouldn't miss this for the world!"

"Cool," said Matthew, echoing Alex's earlier enthusiasm. "The museum closes at five-thirty today. We should go there soon."

"Sounds good," said a voice behind them.

Matthew and Alex both spun around. It was Sally.

"What do you mean?" asked Matthew.

"Sounds good," Sally repeated, as she finished fastening her hair into a ponytail and casually sat down at the table. "I'm coming too."

"What are you talking about?" said Matthew, innocently.

"I heard what you were saying," said Sally. "You want to sneak around after the museum's closed. I wonder what Dad would say."

"He'd say you'd gone nuts," said Alex.

"Alex is right. Dad would never believe you," agreed Matthew smugly.

"Maybe. But I'm sure Mr. Goring would be very interested in hearing about your little adventure yesterday. Perhaps I'll just stop by his office on Monday," said Sally, grinning back at the two of them.

"Okay, okay," said Matthew, over Alex's protests. "You can come too."

Alex did nothing but complain about Sally coming along with them as the three made their way downtown. While they waited at the crossing opposite the museum, Alex let out a sneeze that made everyone stare.

"Are you sure you took some allergy medicine before you left?" said Matthew, anxiously.

"I did," said Alex. "Honest!"

At the same table in the cafeteria where he had spoken with Tess, Matthew reviewed his plan with

Sally and Alex. They would wait until just before closing and then go behind the drapes that Tess had shown him near the mummy case. Then they would hide in the Restoration Room while the guards locked up. From there, they would sneak into the Portrait Gallery.

"But how do we get into the workshop?" asked Sally.

"The back door to the Restoration Room doesn't have a handle. It's always open," explained Matthew. "No problem there. We just have to be careful in case Runsiman comes in to work on the painting."

"Well, if no one notices us now, they can always run the videotape later," said Alex, pointing out a security camera in the ceiling.

"He's right, Matthew," said Sally.

"Don't worry," explained Matthew. "I've been watching the cameras. They do a slow sweep of each room, but never point in the same direction for very long. We should be able to avoid being seen by them."

As the three of them wandered casually through the Egyptian Room, Matthew kept a close eye on the museum guards. Sally seemed genuinely interested in the artefacts on display. Alex sneezed loudly several times, as they wandered around the exhibits.

"I hope you can keep that sneeze under control, Alex," said Matthew when they met up again.

"Yeah," agreed Sally, joining them. "You're a dead give-away. Is this the mummy case?"

Matthew nodded and pointed out the red drapes, behind which lay the secret entrance to the Restoration Room.

"It's five-fifteen," said Matthew, glancing at his watch. "They should make an announcement soon for everyone to leave the museum."

Just then, the fifteen minute warning boomed over the P.A. system. When it got closer to five-thirty, Matthew, Alex and Sally lingered close to the mummy case. A museum guard glanced cursorily at them, before turning to have a word with the woman wiping tables in the cafeteria. As Matthew had predicted, the security camera pointed only briefly at them, then slowly turned away.

"Now!" said Matthew, and they slipped out of sight.

CHAPTER SIX

THE RESTORATION ROOM

Peeking through a small gap in the drapes, Matthew watched the museum guard continue to chat.

By the time he turns around, thought Matthew, *he'll have forgotten all about us.*

"Ouch," whispered Sally.

"Oops," muttered Alex, almost knocking a box off the shelf beside him. "There's not much room in here, you know."

"Just keep your bony elbows to yourself."

"Quit it, you two!" snapped Matthew. Peeking through the gap in the drapes again, he saw another security guard look in the direction of the mummy case.

"Oh no!" whispered Matthew.

"What is it?" asked Sally under her breath.

"One of the guards," answered Matthew. "Coming this way."

All three of them held their breath as the guard sauntered across the exhibit hall, his footsteps echoing on the tiled floor. Then he stopped.

"All clear?" called a voice.

"Guess so," said the first guard. "I thought I heard something."

"Probably nothing," said his colleague. "Time for a break!"

The two guards walked to the exit and switched off the main lights, plunging the windowless room into darkness for a moment before the night-lights came on.

"Close call," Matthew said, turning around. But Alex and Sally were gone. The door at the end of the alcove was ajar, so he followed them into the Restoration Room.

Inside, things were much the same as before. Matthew felt the hair on the back of his neck prickle. He wondered if Alex and Sally felt the same way, but kept his thoughts to himself. The coat rack no longer had Tess's jacket hanging on it, but her coffee mug

43

still sat on the table. Sally was running her hand over a small piece of sculpture.

"Don't touch anything!" Matthew admonished his sister. "We'd better hurry. We don't have much time. The guards are on a break but they'll be making their rounds soon. Where's Alex?"

"Down there!" whispered Sally.

"Wow," came a voice from under a table. "This is certainly weird stuff."

"Alex," asked Matthew, "what are you doing?"

Slowly, Alex got to his feet, clutching the copy of *The Supernatural Revealed.* "This book's pretty cool," he said, skimming the pages. "Maybe there's something in here about your ghost."

"Better not touch anything," repeated Matthew. "Leave it where it was."

"Which way to the Portrait Gallery?" asked Sally, eager to get going.

"Through there," replied Matthew, pointing at the door leading to the museum corridor.

"Hey, what's that in the corner?" asked Alex. "Under that sheet."

"That's the self-portrait of Nicolaas van der Leyden," said Matthew. "But don't mess with it!"

Alex was already in the corner lifting the sheet.

44

"Achoo!"

"Alex!" hissed Matthew and Sally together.

"Sorry," Alex apologized, dropping the white sheet back into place. "My allergy medicine must not have kicked in yet."

"Come on," said Matthew, gesturing to the others.

"Shhh!" Matthew whispered to Sally and Alex as he squinted through a gap in the drapes. He could see two beams of light in the distance.

"The guards are on their way," he warned. "Keep still!"

The beams of light grew larger, then swept along the walls and cases. Matthew couldn't hear what the guards were saying, but they seemed to be searching for something.

"ACHOO!"

This time Alex's sneeze sounded like an explosion. The guards raced toward the mummy case.

"Quick!" whispered Matthew. "Follow me!"

The three of them rushed back into the Restoration Room and went through the door that led to the corridor.

"Looks clear," Matthew said. "Come on."

"Where to?" Sally asked.

"How about the cafeteria?" suggested Alex.

"The cafeteria's closed," snipped Matthew.

"I know," Alex shot back. "But what about the delivery doors?"

"Okay," Matthew said. "Let's go!"

Then a voice shouted, "Stop right there!"

A guard!

"Run!" screamed Sally, sprinting down the corridor, with Alex and Matthew close behind.

"Stop! Come back!" shouted the guard, chasing after them.

"Split up!" ordered Matthew, breathlessly, as he took off down a side corridor with Sally right behind. Glancing over his shoulder, he saw Alex run in the opposite direction.

Stealing along the dark corridor, Matthew kept hearing voices. He and Sally soon reached the Portrait Gallery and halted in front of *The Gloomy Cavalier*.

"What happened to you the last time you were here?" Sally whispered, trying to catch her breath.

"It was weird," said Matthew, panting. "I was standing right here, when I saw him smile. And his eyes moved."

"You mean like that?" choked Sally.

Matthew looked back at the painting. Peter Glimmer's eyes were once again alive. Suddenly a

46

beam of light struck the wall to the left of the painting. A flashlight! One of the security guards had found them! As the guard approached, Matthew grabbed Sally's arm and plunged into the canvas.

CHAPTER SEVEN

IN THE PICTURE

The room was just as Matthew remembered it: the large table with the fruit, the blue flowers and the overturned wineglass. He could see the harbour scene on the far wall. They were inside Peter's portrait.

"Where are we?" asked Sally.

"Don't worry. We're safe," Matthew assured her. "The guards can't find us now."

"You are correct, Matthew," said a voice behind them. "They cannot see you here."

"Who's that?" asked Sally, turning around.

"That is Peter Glimmer," said Matthew.

"I am so glad you came back," said Peter, moving closer, the air rippling as he did. "But you are not alone."

"This is my sister, Sally. We had to get away from the guards," said Matthew.

"Yes," said Peter. "I need your help, before it is too late."

"What's he talking about, Matthew?" Sally asked, looking at Peter from behind her brother's back.

"That's what I came here to figure out," declared Matthew. "What is the rest of your story?"

"Pay close attention," Peter said.

He gently waved his hand and the animals carved on the frame began to writhe. It no longer showed a view out into the gallery. Instead, they were looking at the image of a man painting in a studio.

"This is Amsterdam, 1666," said Peter. "To you this is the distant past."

The air shimmered as Peter paced around the room.

"My father was an artist," Peter continued, "but he was also an alchemist. My mother died when I was a baby. My father brought me up alone, and often allowed me to help him in his laboratory. His work led him to the study of medicine, and, after my mother died, he devoted more and more time to medical research. He hunted tirelessly for a cure for the disease that killed her."

The scenes in the frame swirled and changed as Peter told his story.

"But where does your uncle fit into all this?" Matthew interrupted.

"Nicolaas van der Leyden and my father were brothers-in-law, and studied art and alchemy together for many years," Peter replied. "They were also very learned in magic. As my father became more focused on medicine, his relationship with my uncle grew increasingly strained. There were many disagreements. One night, I witnessed a fierce quarrel between them."

Matthew and Sally watched as Peter's father and Nicolaas van der Leyden argued vehemently. With a start, Matthew recognised one of the men.

"Hey, that's Mr. Runsiman!" Matthew exclaimed.

Peter agreed, "It is."

"Who's Mr. Runsiman?" whispered Sally.

"He's the curator of the museum," Matthew answered.

Peter went on. "Not long after that, my father mysteriously disappeared. I never saw him again, and Nicolaas van der Leyden became my guardian."

"What happened to your father?" asked Sally.

"I shall get to that soon," Peter answered. "As I grew older, my uncle grew obsessed with his experiments. He often asked me what I remembered about my father's formulae. I did not find out why until later. He instructed me in alchemy and magic too. He needed an assistant, and I now know that he hoped to initiate me into the black arts. However, he did not tell me everything he knew. There was one spell book that I was forbidden to read.

"On my thirteenth birthday, a small wooden chest arrived for me while my uncle was out of the house. Inside, I found pieces of wood carved with unicorns, dragons, gryphons and other unusual creatures. At the bottom of the chest lay a sealed letter, addressed to me. It was from my father. It explained that the wooden carvings, when put together, would form..."

"A frame?" Matthew finished the sentence for him.

"Exactly," said Peter. "Following the instructions in the letter, I built the frame you see before you. The moment it took shape, I watched in amazement as my father's face appeared."

"So your father was a prisoner as well?" asked Matthew.

"No, Matthew," Peter went on. "This was merely an image. When I reached out to touch his face, all the colours swirled together. When I withdrew my hand, my father reappeared and spoke. He began by telling me that, if I had received the chest, then my uncle, Nicolaas van der Leyden, had probably murdered him. He needed my help to bring van der Leyden to justice."

Matthew couldn't believe it. "Mr. Runsiman killed your father?"

"Indeed."

"What else did he tell you?"

"My father explained that, before I was born, he had come across an old sailor at the waterfront. The sailor gave my father some curious wooden carvings, which he said came from the South Seas. My father later put the pieces together to make a frame, and was astonished to see the old sailor appear inside it. The sailor told him to keep the frame in a safe place, for my father would need it some day to avert a great disaster. The image in the frame then changed to show fleeting images of the future, before going blank.

"Over the next few years, my father studied the frame, and discovered that it could be used as a portal through time. If someone's portrait was placed inside the frame, that person would be able to travel to any time and place where the portrait had ever been. Once he determined this, he hid the pieces and

52

waited for the right time. In his message to me, he made it clear that I was to use the frame to fulfil the mission entrusted to him. He knew by then that my uncle would be responsible for the chaotic future he'd been shown by the old sailor."

"What exactly is your uncle capable of? Can he really be that dangerous?" asked Matthew, still sceptical.

"It has to do with my father's most important discovery: the formula for a magic paint. If this magic paint is used to create a person's portrait, it gives that person eternal life, provided the portrait is kept in good condition through continual restoration. My father was elated at the prospect of being able to use this power for the benefit of mankind. Before he realised how evil my uncle was, he hoped that one day the two of them might be able to discover cures for all the diseases that plague mankind."

"That would have been so cool," breathed Sally.

Peter went on. "One winter, while my uncle was travelling through Egypt in search of spells, my father used the magic paint to create a double portrait of himself and his brother-in-law."

"Is that the painting that's in the Restoration Room? The one that's supposed to be a self-portrait of van der Leyden?" Matthew asked. He remembered Tess saying that it might once have been a double portrait.

"It is," said Peter. "When my uncle returned from Egypt, the arguments between him and my father began to turn bitter. My father suspected that van der Leyden was dabbling in black magic. Before he dared to tell my uncle about the magic paint and the double portrait, he had to be sure of my uncle's integrity. My father decided to look at his brother-in-law's spell book to see what he had been studying.

"Using his own magic, my father located the book and pored over it. To his horror, all of its spells were for black magic. It was obvious that van der Leyden had become, in fact, a master of the black arts. His notes revealed that his trip to Egypt had been part of his search for the secret to eternal life, the legendary Philosopher's Stone. He intended to use his powers to rule the world, forever. He had not yet found a way to gain immortality, but his knowledge was growing daily.

"When he read this, my father was appalled at the thought that his own discovery would enable van der Leyden to carry out his diabolical plot. He knew that he had to destroy the magic paint, all his notes about the formula, the double portrait, and the spell book.

"He was able to get rid of all of the magic paint, and most of his own notes. He began to scrape away some of my uncle's image from the portrait, but my uncle interrupted him before he could finish. He could not get to the spell book before he was killed."

"What happened?" asked Sally.

"When my uncle walked in on my father that night, he saw enough of my father's last remaining notes to understand what my father was doing, and he instantly realised that the magic paint was the key to fulfilling his evil plan. My father insisted that my uncle would never achieve immortality, because he had destroyed the paint. My father also made it clear that he would never reveal its formula.

"They fought. My uncle wrested the damaged portrait and his spell book away from my father. He then ran to the attic and locked the door with a powerful spell. When my father realised that he could not break the spell, he used his magic to leave me the message in the frame. He had to act quickly. When his message was complete, he went to his lawyer's house and told him to give me the chest when I was thirteen, for he knew my uncle would have his revenge."

Matthew tried to digest this information. He asked, "Did you ever discover what happened to your father?"

"Yes. I used the frame to figure out what happened, after I was trapped here. Let me show you."

The scene in the frame changed once more, to show Johan Glimmer walking into the attic. As soon as he crossed the threshold, he was frozen in place while van der Leyden held him at bay with an out-stretched hand. The double portrait stood on an easel between them. With a sweep of his arm, van der Leyden hurled Glimmer into his half of the portrait. As van der Leyden's hand came down, Johan Glimmer's image vanished from the canvas.

Peter broke the silence. "My father was trapped in his self-portrait in the same way that I would be. When my uncle wiped it clean, my father was lost for-ever. He tried to do the same to me, but I was pro-tected by the magic frame."

"Peter, I'm so sorry," murmured Matthew.

"Thank you, Matthew." Peter sighed. "Of course I did not know exactly what had happened when I received my father's instructions. I did know, howev-er, that I was the only one who could stop my uncle from carrying out his evil plan. After my father's image faded, I took the frame apart. I then put the pieces back into the chest and hid the chest beneath my bed, until I could decide what further action to take.

"How can you do anything if you're stuck in this frame?" asked Matthew.

"That is why I brought you here," replied Peter. "With your help, I may be able to stop my uncle from succeeding."

"How?" asked Sally.

Peter continued. "You will recall that this frame acts as a portal to times that occur after the completion of the portrait placed within it. In his message to me, my father told me that the frame could also be used to travel to times *before* the creation of the portrait, but only if a particular spell were used. That spell was one of many in my uncle's book.

"My father told me where my uncle hid his spell book. He then instructed me to find the right spell, and to study the book in order to gain the powers I would need to defeat my uncle. I also needed to create a self-portrait to place within the frame, so that I could use the time portal."

"But everyone thinks your uncle painted your portrait," Matthew interrupted.

"Yes. Like the rest of my story, that truth has been hidden for centuries."

"What did your father expect you to do?" asked Sally.

"My father wanted me to go back to a time before his death, so that the two of us would be able to thwart my uncle before he became powerful."

Matthew and Sally looked at each other as they took this in.

"So what exactly is your plan now? How do we fit into it?" asked Matthew.

"Without you, my plan cannot work. Let me explain."

CHAPTER EIGHT

PETER'S PLAN

"Once I had seen my father's message, I knew why my uncle asked me so many questions about my father's work. He thought I might know the formula for the magic paint. Of course, I could not know anything about it, before I had seen my father's message. But my uncle could not know that. I now believe that my uncle intended to try to lure me into joining him in his evil work.

"I first decided to begin painting my self-portrait, after the style taught to me by both my father and my uncle."

"That's why they think van der Leyden painted it!" exclaimed Matthew.

"Yes. My uncle approved of my efforts. He thought that my skills might lead to commissions that could support him while he studied magic.

"The second thing I had to do was find the forbidden book."

The frame now showed Peter alone in the attic. Matthew and Sally saw him slowly ease a cabinet away from the wall to reveal a small wooden panel in the brickwork. Peter pushed against a brick, which swung inward. He reached inside and pulled out a key. Then he unlocked the wooden panel. He removed two books and took them to the table. At that point, the image froze and the carvings on the frame stopped moving.

"One of those books was my uncle's medical journal," explained Peter. "The other was decorated with symbols and inscriptions which I had never seen before. It contained hundreds of enchantments, curses and spells.

"My uncle was often out of the house during the day and, while he was gone, I took the opportunity to study that book. I spent months acquiring mystical powers, trying in vain to uncover the time travel spell. Eventually I became adept at working many of the most powerful incantations. I was even able to transform my hand into a white-hot flame, and direct it at a target."

The scenes in the frame began to change again, as Peter's story continued.

"I had to keep my activities hidden from my uncle until I could finish my portrait. When it was finally completed, I put it into the mysterious frame and hung it on the studio wall. I still needed to discover the proper spell, which would open the time portal. Luckily, my uncle never noticed anything unusual about the frame.

"By then, life with my uncle had become unbearable. His medical work was becoming more and more depraved. All sorts of sinister and unsavoury people came to visit him at the house. One of these was Samuel Valkenburg, the chief jailer at the Amsterdam prison. He supplied my uncle with the unclaimed bodies of executed prisoners for his research. Valkenburg also helped him to procure bodies in other ways. I overheard them discussing a plan to rob graves, and I also heard rumours in the market about beggars disappearing without a trace."

So Tess was right, thought Matthew, remembering their conversation in the cafeteria.

The picture in the frame suddenly turned entirely black. Peter turned to them with a grave expression.

"Even so, I was not prepared for the worst of it. One day, my uncle asked me to accompany him to Valkenburg's to fetch a new corpse. When we got there, I was stunned when the man's body we were lifting suddenly opened its eyes. The man was still alive! He grabbed my wrist and begged for mercy. Before I had a chance to intervene, my uncle killed him with a swift blow to the head. There was nothing I could do to stop it."

Once more, the frame began to depict Peter's story as he spoke.

"Horrified, I ran out into the back alley. But before I could make my escape, I felt a sharp blow to the back of my head and everything went dark. I woke up on the floor of the attic laboratory. On the table next to me lay the man my uncle had murdered. I tried the door, but it was locked. I tried to blast it open with the white flame, but my powers were of no use. My uncle's magic kept me trapped in the room."

"But the spell book was in there with you. Couldn't you find the time travel spell?" asked Sally.

"I did. But I did not have time to learn it before my uncle returned. Nor was I able to find a spell to help me break out of the locked attic."

Peter changed the scene in the frame again. This time, Nicolaas van der Leyden stood in the doorway of the attic laboratory, glaring at his nephew, who sat at a table with the forbidden book open in front of him.

"When my uncle saw me with his book, he was enraged. He tried to kill me, but I fought back with my own powers. A desperate battle followed, but I was no match for him. What saved me, in the end, was the smoke from the fire."

Matthew and Sally watched as van der Leyden's hand was suddenly transformed into a white-hot flame. Peter retaliated with fire, and the attic became engulfed in flames. As smoke filled the burning room, van der Leyden doubled over, coughing. Peter took his chance to escape, and staggered out the door.

"Though I escaped downstairs to the studio," said Peter, "my uncle was right behind me."

Matthew and Sally both flinched, as they watched the studio door being blown off its hinges. The force of the blast thrust Peter against the wall. Then van der Leyden waved his hand, and Peter was launched into the air right at them. Matthew and Sally raised their arms in front of their faces to protect themselves, but all they could see was the cruel face of Nicolaas van der Leyden staring directly at them.

"What's going on?" said Matthew. "What happened?"

"I lost the battle, Matthew," replied Peter, "and this portrait limbo was the result. You are looking at the moment that I was imprisoned inside this very painting. My uncle caught me before I had time to learn the time travel spell. Now that I am trapped here by his black magic, I am unable to use the frame to travel back through time and help my father."

"But why would van der Leyden trap you in here if he knew it was a time portal?" Sally asked.

"You must remember that my uncle had no idea that the frame was magical," said Peter.

"Why didn't he destroy the painting once he'd trapped you inside?" asked Matthew.

"He has tried, many times. He killed my father that way, and he thought he could do the same to me. But the frame has protected my portrait from my uncle's magic for centuries. Although he knows now that the frame possesses strong magic, he does not realise that I am still alive."

"But how can you stay alive for so long without food or water?" Sally asked, aghast at what Peter's life must be like.

"I do not experience time in the same way as you. I can view any manner of things that are happening, but, for me, only a few moments have actually passed since I was imprisoned."

Sally went pale. She grabbed Matthew's wrist tightly as she asked, "Does that mean that we're trapped here, too?"

"No. You are quite safe. My uncle's spell applies only to me. It was my magic that brought you here, and he has no way of knowing what I plan to do."

"Wait a minute. How has your uncle stayed alive all this time? Is it because his portrait made with the magic paint is still around?" asked Matthew.

"Yes," said Peter, "my uncle was able to save the portion with his own image. He has guarded it closely for more than three centuries. He also kept my self-portrait, until he lost it during the chaos of the Russian Revolution. He needs to enter his own portrait from time to time, to replenish his life force."

"Like a vampire going back to his coffin," said Sally with a shudder.

Matthew recalled Tess telling him how Runsiman worked alone late into the night.

"What has he been doing for the past three hundred years?" Matthew asked Peter. "How did he end up in the museum, as curator?"

Peter's hand swiftly passed over the frame once again. The strange animals began to writhe as the colours swirled. Matthew and Sally could see a man wearing a long, pale green jacket over a white shirt with frills at the cuffs. Although he wore a white wig with a short ponytail, it was clearly Nicolaas van der Leyden. Matthew recognised his clothes as belonging to the time of the French Revolution. Van der Leyden was sitting at the laboratory bench, feverishly scribbling in a thick notebook.

Then the scene shifted to a beautiful white house with a wide veranda. Several elegantly dressed women, accompanied by men in grey military uniforms, strolled in the foreground. Sally pointed at one of the men, and sure enough, Matthew saw that it was van der Leyden again. Peter explained how this house also contained a laboratory where his uncle worked, night after night, on his quest for the formula that would give him eternal life.

Then the picture changed to what Matthew realised was Russia. He could see a whitewashed church with gleaming gold domes. Light snow fell on a large square surrounded by grand buildings, reminding Matthew of the museum. The focus shifted to the interior of one of the buildings. Nicolaas van der Leyden, dressed in clothes that Matthew guessed dated from the early part of the twentieth century, was again working furiously in a laboratory. This time he was using electricity. Sparks flew. Then the image froze, and the figures on the frame stopped moving.

"So you see," said Peter, "while I have been trapped here in this painting, my uncle has been alive for over three hundred years. After our battle in the studio, he left Amsterdam. He settled in Paris, until the French Revolution forced him to flee to America. The American Civil War forced him to move again. He was in Russia in 1917, when yet another revolution almost deprived him of his portrait. That was when the two paintings were separated from one another. He returned to America and began working in museums and galleries, where he could care for his own portrait and perhaps recover mine, as well.

"My uncle has never given up searching for the formula. The portrait's enchantment requires restoration with the magic paint if it is to give immortality. Naturally, the paint on the canvas has deteriorated, and the portrait has been damaged by fire several times. His powers have slowly been eroded as the painting's condition has worsened over the years. Without a fresh supply of the magic paint, my uncle has continued to age, albeit at a much slower rate than other men. However, in the guise of Albert Runsiman, Nicolaas van der Leyden is now in the process of fully restoring his portrait."

"What do you mean? He hasn't discovered the formula for the paint, has he?" asked Sally.

"I have been watching his activities through the ages, using the frame. Unfortunately, he has indeed finally succeeded in recreating the formula, and he has almost finished the restoration."

"But what does that mean?" said Sally.

"That the world is about to change dramatically for the worse," said Peter. "See for yourself."

Peter waved his hand once more. And once more, the strange figures began to twist. The frame now showed a series of nightmare scenarios. A city lay in ruins. The devastation was like the aftermath of a horrific war. Matthew and Sally saw hundreds of people filing into the doorway of an enormous building that had the letters NVDL etched into its stonework. Columns of people in ragged clothes passed by a colossal stone statue of Nicolaas van der Leyden.

"This is what's going to happen, isn't it?" Matthew whispered.

"Yes," confirmed Peter. "Unless you can stop it."

"But what can we do?" Sally wondered aloud.

"The spell book," Peter said simply. "I had to leave it behind. I first need to find the spell which will break the enchantment that has trapped me in this portrait. Then I can learn and apply the time travel spell that I found the night I was imprisoned."

"But the book is back in 1666, isn't it?" said Matthew.

Peter's eyes locked on Matthew's face. "Since I cannot go myself, I need to send you both back into the past to retrieve the book for me. Although I am trapped here, I can open the portal for you and Sally to travel to a time shortly after my uncle imprisoned me. You must move quickly once you are there. Will you help me?"

Matthew thought for a moment. "I don't see that there's much choice, if that vision of the future is really true. Sally," he said, turning to her, "you should go home and let me handle this. I'd rather you were safe."

"None of us is safe if you fail, Matthew," she replied solemnly. "You might need some help."

Matthew and Sally looked once more at each other, reached out to clasp hands, then turned to nod at Peter.

"Very well," said Peter.

The images in the frame began to move again, and the colours in the picture swirled around like a whirlpool. Matthew and Sally were pulled backwards into the frame. "Wait! We don't speak the language!" blurted Matthew.

"I have taken care of that," said Peter, as he faded from their sight. Then the room was gone.

CHAPTER NINE

THE FORBIDDEN BOOK

Matthew and Sally stepped out from the portrait of Peter Glimmer into Nicolaas van der Leyden's studio, in the Amsterdam of 1666. Beside them was a wooden table, in the middle of which stood the vase of blue flowers. Matthew turned to see the painting of Peter Glimmer, perched on an easel. The paint shone as if still wet, and the colours were more vivid than he remembered them being. The frame looked exactly the same as when he had seen it in the museum.

Matthew could see the harbour clearly from the studio window. He stretched his hand through the window, half expecting the whole scene to shimmer before his eyes, but he felt fresh air. He gazed over the rooftops at the masts of the Dutch fleet. Below were warehouses, with men hard at work unloading crates and boxes from the ships. Nearby was a crowded marketplace with people strolling from stall to stall. Matthew could hear merchants calling out their wares. Seagulls swooped overhead, attracted by the smell of fresh fish. Carriages and men on horseback wove through the cobblestone streets, the horses' hooves clip-clopping as they passed. Matthew was amazed that he could understand Dutch being shouted in the marketplace below.

"We have to find the spell book," he whispered to his sister. "There's no telling when Peter's uncle will be home. Let's go to the attic quickly."

They stepped out from the studio into a narrow, winding staircase.

"Come on," said Matthew, gesturing to Sally.

Matthew led the way up to the attic. The door creaked slightly as he opened it. Walls were lined with shelves containing beakers and all kinds of strange equipment. Matthew winced when he saw two blood-stained tables in the corner. Through the attic window, Matthew looked again at the city below. Canals wound this way and that before reaching the sea.

In the centre of the room stood a high stool and another table. On the table was a lit candle. "He must be coming back soon if he left this burning," Matthew said to Sally. "Let's find that book and get out of here!"

"Matthew!" Sally called, pointing at a cabinet by the window. "That must be it! Let's move it out of the way," she said, gripping the cabinet with both hands. "This thing's heavy!"

Together they slid the cabinet away from the wall, revealing a small wooden door in the brickwork.

"Which brick was it?" Matthew asked his sister.

"I didn't notice. Just try them all," replied Sally.

Matthew pressed various bricks until one swung inward, revealing the small chamber. Reaching inside, he pulled out a large iron key. "Got it!"

He put the key into the lock in the wooden door. It turned easily. Matthew opened the door, reached in and pulled out one of two books.

"The forbidden book!" he announced triumphantly. "We've got what we came for. Let's go, before..."

BANG!

Matthew and Sally both turned their heads as the attic door slammed back against the wall.

Nicolaas van der Leyden stood in the doorway.

"I thought I heard voices," he growled. "Who are you? Friends of Peter's? And so strangely dressed."

Matthew and Sally recognised Samuel Valkenburg towering behind van der Leyden. Both men were staring at the spell book in Matthew's hand.

"Get rid of them!" hissed Valkenburg.

"Of course," agreed van der Leyden in a menacing tone. "I do not think we have to worry about a shortage of bodies for my next experiment."

Matthew's heart pounded as he frantically scanned the attic for a way to escape.

"Run!" he shouted to Sally.

Matthew headed for the door, but Valkenburg grabbed him with giant hands. Matthew felt as if he was going to be crushed as the huge man lifted him off the floor, his legs kicking wildly in the air. As Valkenburg's grip tightened, Matthew dropped the book. Desperate, Matthew stretched his fingers towards the candle on the table and manoeuvred the flame against Valkenburg's hand. He yelped with pain and dropped Matthew, giving him a chance to break free and run for the door. Looking back, Matthew could see that van der Leyden had Sally pinned with a spell. Light flashed from an emerald ring on van der Leyden's left hand. It was the same ring that Matthew had seen Runsiman wearing.

Matthew knew he was powerless against the alchemist's black magic. Valkenburg, now recovered, lunged at Matthew again.

I have to get help, thought Matthew, terrified.

He scurried down the stairs, stumbling into the studio one floor below. He slammed the door and rammed a chair up against the handle.

That should buy me some time, he thought. But time for what? If he succeeded in reaching the streets, he had no idea where to go. Even if he went to the authorities, who would ever believe him?

The portrait of Peter Glimmer sat on its easel by the window. In the corner stood another painting. *Maybe I should just destroy van der Leyden's portrait now and get it over with!* thought Matthew.

Before he could do anything, he heard a series of loud crashes, as one wooden panel of the studio door after another was shattered by an axe. Without thinking, Matthew dashed to the portrait of Peter Glimmer, sank his hand into the canvas and was gone.

CHAPTER TEN

SALLY WHO?

"Sally's trapped!" shouted Matthew, as he reappeared inside Peter Glimmer's portrait. "You have to help her!"

"Something has gone terribly wrong," said Peter, breathing heavily. Sweat stood out on his forehead, and he grasped the table edge for balance.

The carvings on the frame moved in a blur around the portrait. Peter became harder and harder to see, as the colours inside the portrait began to swirl and mingle.

"What's happening?" shouted Matthew.

The room began to resemble a chalk drawing in the rain.

"The time stream has been altered," Matthew heard Peter gasp. "I could not foresee this. I need to regain control of the portal, but I can't keep you in here while I do that. Come back as soon as you can," said Peter, as he struggled to raise his arm.

"But what about Sally?" insisted Matthew. "I can't just leave her! You have to..."

Matthew found himself back in the gallery, gaping at the portrait. This time he saw no hint of life in Peter Glimmer's face; the portal was closed. Looking down, Matthew noticed there was gold and blue paint on his hands. He had to find Alex. And fast.

Checking his watch, Matthew realised that hardly any time had passed while he had been inside the painting. As he hurried along the corridors, he saw no sign of the museum's guards, and soon reached the cafeteria.

"Psst!"

Matthew saw Alex's head protruding above the counter beside the coffee machine.

"What did you do?" said Alex, as Matthew crouched down next to him. "Try your hand at painting?"

Matthew looked down and saw that his shirt and jeans were also splattered with paint.

"It's a long story," said Matthew. "Have you seen Sally?"

"Sally?" said Alex. "Sally who?"

"My sister, Sally!" repeated Matthew. "Have you seen her?"

"Long lost sister, I presume," said Alex, looking puzzled.

"Stop it!" Matthew snapped. "You know who I mean! Sally!"

Alex is such a clown, he thought.

"This place has made your brain fuzzy," said Alex. "You know that you haven't got a sister. Are you okay?"

From the expression on his face, Matthew could tell that Alex was being sincere. "Uh, fine. Just fine," he replied slowly.

The reason for Alex's confusion finally dawned on Matthew. Peter had said that the time stream was altered. Matthew and Sally's journey back to 1666, and their encounter with Nicolaas van der Leyden in the attic, had somehow changed the present. Sally was lost in the past.

I have to save her somehow! thought Matthew.

"So what's with the paint?" Alex asked him.

"Like I said, it's a long story," said Matthew. "We'd better get out of here fast!"

"The service entrance is through here," said Alex. "Near the refrigerators."

"Then we'd better get going right away, before our luck runs out," urged Matthew.

The two boys pushed open the service entrance door, setting off a piercing alarm. They ran as far from the museum as they could before stopping for breath.

"So what did happen to you?" asked Alex, his chest heaving.

"Let's catch that bus!" said Matthew. "I'll tell you everything on the way home."

When they got back to Matthew's house, Matthew saw that all the pictures of Sally were missing. Family pictures showed Matthew alone with his parents. He raced upstairs into what had once been Sally's room and instead found a home office. Her closet contained no clothes, just shelf after shelf of books beside a filing cabinet. When Matthew's parents eventually returned home, they didn't mention Sally. Sally was gone, or rather, had never existed.

Matthew and Alex sat up late into the night talking. Matthew was at last able to convince his friend that he was telling the truth, and not losing his mind. He made Alex swear not to say anything to anyone about what had happened, until he could figure out what to do.

When he woke up the next morning, Matthew almost didn't remember Sally himself. His memories of her were dim, like a fading dream. He struggled to keep an image of her face in his mind. He knew that it was up to him to rescue her from the past.

After breakfast, Alex went home, giving Matthew the thumbs up as he left. Matthew hoped he could trust his friend to keep his secret.

Alone in his room, Matthew wracked his brains trying to figure out a way to save Sally. Even if he didn't understand how it was possible, he did know now that Nicolaas van der Leyden was the same person as the museum curator, Albert Runsiman. Matthew reached for the phone, pulled a business card from his pocket and punched in the number.

"Tess," he said, "I need to see you."

CHAPTER ELEVEN

CONVINCING TESS

Matthew told his parents he had some research to do at the city library, but instead headed downtown to a coffee shop near the museum.

"This had better be good," said Tess, as she sat down across from him.

"I couldn't talk to you on the phone," said Matthew.

"So, what's the big mystery?" Tess asked, stirring her coffee. "And why are we meeting here? Couldn't you have come to the museum?"

"I may have a problem visiting the museum after what happened," Matthew replied.

"What do you mean?"

"Last night some guards caught Alex, Sally and me in the museum after hours. We stayed behind to learn more about the van der Leyden paintings."

"Jeez, Matthew!" said Tess, leaning back in her chair. "If I knew you were planning a stunt like that, I'd never have shown you around."

"I must admit, you were a great help," said Matthew. "Especially showing me that secret passage behind the mummy case!"

"Oh, this is great, just great. I could lose my job over this, Matthew!" exclaimed Tess, pushing her chair back angrily and standing up. "I'm out of here!"

"Wait," said Matthew. "I met him."

"Who?" asked Tess.

"Peter Glimmer."

"Peter Glimmer?" said Tess, shaking her head. "What are you talking about?"

"The sort of things you told me about in the cafeteria," said Matthew. "Remember?"

"You shouldn't let all that stuff go to your head, Matthew," said Tess, beginning to move toward the door.

"I'm telling you, I met him," repeated Matthew, firmly. "I travelled back in time to 1666."

"This is crazy," said Tess, but she looked a little curious.

"At least listen to what I have to say," insisted Matthew, "before you make up your mind."

Tess hesitated for a moment, then sat back down. Matthew told her almost everything that had happened at the museum: his first encounter with Peter Glimmer on the school visit, their next meeting when Peter had explained everything about his father, the magical frame, the threat Nicolaas van der Leyden posed, and finally the trip into the past to try to retrieve the spell book. For the most part, Tess sat calmly and listened, occasionally asking Matthew to clarify something. Much to Matthew's relief, Tess didn't seem to think he was crazy. She seemed to believe every word, except for one thing.

"When we first met, you told me you didn't have any brothers or sisters," said Tess. "Who's Sally?"

Matthew didn't remember any such conversation, but realised it was the change in the time stream playing tricks again.

"My sister," said Matthew, "came with me into the past. But things didn't work out as Peter had planned. I managed to escape, but I had to leave Sally behind. She may even have been killed. Everything was changed when I came back. Now no one else, not even my parents, knows that she ever existed. I have to try really hard to remember her myself."

"Why do you think she may have been killed?" Tess asked.

"She was captured by Nicolaas van der Leyden," explained Matthew. "He's Mr. Runsiman."

Tess stared at him, open-mouthed. "What?"

"Runsiman *is* Nicolaas van der Leyden," said Matthew. "He's still alive after all these centuries, still working to take over the world, just like Peter Glimmer told me."

"That's just too crazy," insisted Tess, her eyes widening.

"It's all true. You've got to believe me," Matthew said. "You told me yourself that van der Leyden was rumoured to have been involved in magic."

"Well, yes," Tess began, "but…"

Matthew cut her off. "When I saw him in 1666, he didn't have that scar over his left eye that Mr. Runsiman has. But he did have the same ring with the green gemstone. You must have noticed that."

"I have noticed it," Tess started to say, "but that doesn't mean…"

"And you said Mr. Runsiman always insists on working on the portrait alone and at night. You yourself called the picture spooky. You said you once felt that it was watching you."

"Hold on, hold on," Tess said, raising her hand and spilling her coffee. "You seriously believe this stuff, don't you?"

"At first I wasn't sure what to think," said Matthew. "I just knew it wasn't a dream. Trust me. I met Peter Glimmer, and the past is very real. I must find a way to rescue Sally."

"What do you propose?"

"You need to help me get back into the museum without being seen," said Matthew.

"Hold on, Matthew," said Tess. "I'm not sure if I should get involved in this."

"This morning's perfect," persisted Matthew. "It won't take long."

Tess sighed in defeat. "Okay," she acquiesced, "Mr. Runsiman never comes in on Sundays. It's a good thing that the museum has short hours today." She shook her head. "I should have my head examined for doing this. Come on. My car's parked around the back."

Tess's car turned out to be a Volkswagen Beetle. Its yellow paint was peppered with hundreds of rust spots.

"How old is this thing?" asked Matthew, struggling to fasten the old-fashioned seat belt.

"It was my grandfather's," said Tess, proudly, as she put the key in the ignition. "Ready?"

The car roared noisily to life. Matthew couldn't hear himself think above the rattle of the engine as they drove away.

Just as they were pulling into the museum's underground parking, Tess grabbed Matthew's shoulder and shoved him down roughly. "Runsiman's just leaving! Keep out of sight!" she hissed. Matthew could see Tess wave and hear the engine of another car as it passed them on its way out. "He must have been here all night," Tess muttered, as her car shuddered to a stop. "You can sit up now."

"I'll get you in through the staff entrance before the museum officially opens," continued Tess, as they walked over to the elevators.

She swiped her employee pass and the doors opened.

"If you get caught, don't come running to the Restoration Room," Tess warned. The two of them stepped inside, and she pushed the button for the main floor. "You're strictly on your own. Got it?"

"Okay," said Matthew.

The elevator doors opened directly across from the museum's administration area. Matthew could see that the door to Mr. Runsiman's office was shut tight.

"No one's in yet," said Tess, looking at her watch. "I'll come with you as far as Peter Glimmer's portrait."

"Doesn't look alive to me," said Tess.

Matthew reached out and touched the canvas. He pulled his hand away as if he'd received an electric shock. There was paint on his fingers.

"What's the matter?" asked Tess.

"The canvas is wet," said Matthew. "See for yourself."

"That's odd," said Tess. She lightly touched the same corner Matthew had. "Feels dry to me."

"But look," said Matthew, showing Tess the paint on his fingers.

"Are you sure that paint is from the painting?" asked Tess, with a frown.

"You don't believe me, do you?" said Matthew, annoyed. "The paint was wet."

Matthew reached out his hand again to prove his point. This time it sank deep into the portrait, right up to his elbow.

"Oh my..." stammered Tess.

"When this happened before," said Matthew, "I was pulled into the painting by Peter Glimmer."

"What the..." gasped Tess, alarmed.

"Wish me luck!" said Matthew as he was sucked into the canvas.

CHAPTER TWELVE

THE RESCUE

I'm starting to get used to this, thought Matthew, as he entered the painted room.

Gazing out into the gallery, Matthew saw Tess, still staring at the portrait.

"Matthew," said Peter's voice behind him.

"I don't have time to talk," said Matthew curtly. "I have to save Sally and get the spell book. How does this thing work?"

Peter walked over to the frame and slowly waved his hand across the surface. The strange figures began to move and the paint in the portrait began to swirl, as if he were twirling his fingers in a pool of water. Once the ripples disappeared, Matthew was no longer looking out into the museum. The frame now held a picture of the Amsterdam studio in 1666. Without thinking, and without saying another word to Peter, Matthew jumped into the frame.

Matthew stumbled back into Nicolaas van der Leyden's studio. It was dark outside. The city of Amsterdam was very still, illuminated by a full moon. He hoped he wasn't too late to save Sally. The studio door, now hanging by only one hinge, was splintered with telltale axe marks.

Matthew heard noises coming from the attic. He walked gingerly through the doorway and crept slowly up the stairs. The voice of Nicolaas van der Leyden floated down to him. At the top of the stairs, Matthew pushed the attic door slightly ajar. He could see Sally lying on one of the two tables in the corner. There were no ropes binding her, but she seemed to be frozen to the table.

The spell book was still on the floor.

He's still got her under a spell, thought Matthew.

Sally's mouth was moving but she made no sound. Matthew watched in horror as van der Leyden approached the table, brandishing a long knife. Matthew flung the door wide open and launched himself directly at him. The alchemist lurched backwards, struggling to regain his footing. Matthew then grabbed a bowl filled with red powder and threw it in his face. Instinctively, van der Leyden moved his hands to his eyes and dropped his knife. At the same time, the spell restraining Sally was lifted, and she jumped from the table.

"Run!" Matthew yelled, grabbing the spell book. "I'll hold him off."

Sally mouthed something in reply, but she still couldn't speak.

"Just go!" said Matthew. "I'll be right behind you."

Matthew spun around to see van der Leyden coming at him with a cleaver. He dodged, stumbling as its blade sank into the surface of a table.

"You are trying my patience, boy!" van der Leyden bellowed. "I don't know who you are, but you will pay for this!"

Van der Leyden grabbed another knife and slashed repeatedly at Matthew, forcing him backwards, until he was pressed against a wall.

"It seems your luck has run out," said Nicolaas van der Leyden.

Van der Leyden's hand held Matthew's throat tightly, choking him. Matthew could feel the alchemist's emerald ring press into his skin. As van der Leyden drew back his knife, Matthew clutched the spell book tightly to his chest for protection. Then he heard a muffled thud and the grip around his throat loosened. Sally was standing behind van der Leyden, holding a heavy brass candlestick. Blood poured out of van der Leyden's scalp and he staggered, stunned by Sally's blow.

"Run!" yelled Matthew, still holding the spell book, "I'll jump into the painting right after you!"

Taking advantage of her opponent's momentary weakness, Sally dashed through the attic door and down the stairs, with Matthew close behind.

As they burst into the studio, Matthew shouted out, "Quick! Jump into the painting!" And she disappeared into the canvas, with her brother following closely behind.

Once inside the painting, Matthew was startled to find that nothing was the same. Sally was gone and so was Peter. The frame no longer showed a view into the Portrait Gallery. Instead there was a maelstrom of swiftly moving images, like videotape on fast forward. Matthew guessed that the chaos created in the time stream had somehow affected the images in the frame. The scenes were moving too quickly for Matthew to make sense out of them. Straining his eyes to catch the right moment, Matthew walked slowly toward the frame once more. Still gripping the spell book tightly, he stepped into the whirlpool.

CHAPTER THIRTEEN

MATTHEW KEEPS HIS HEAD

Matthew rolled out onto a wooden floor. He wasn't back in the museum or in Amsterdam. He found himself in a lavishly decorated room. It looked as if someone was getting ready to move. Half-filled crates were everywhere. Paintings, clocks and clothing were scattered around the room. One painting, however, was not packed away. It was the van der Leyden portrait, mounted high on the wall above the fireplace.

An excellent likeness, thought Matthew, having just seen van der Leyden at extremely close quarters. It was strange to think that this was very same portrait as the one in the museum's Restoration Room.

But where is Sally? Matthew thought, surveying his surroundings. His sister was nowhere to be seen. Fear gripped him. It occurred to him that, if she'd also experienced the jumbled up images in the frame, she could be anywhere in time.

Matthew got to his feet and crossed the room to the nearest window. He saw that the street below was thronged with hundreds of people waving red, white and blue flags. He could hear the windows beneath the balcony being smashed repeatedly, and realised that the mob was trying to break in.

The crowd was crushed up against two huge iron gates, which were beginning to buckle. In the courtyard, servants frantically packed boxes into waiting carriages. The scene below reminded Matthew of a movie he'd once seen, and he realised where he was.

I'm in Paris during the French Revolution! thought Matthew in horror.

"Quickly, François!" said a voice from outside the room. "We must load the last few chests into the carriage."

"My lord, there is no time," replied another. "The mob is at the gates. At any moment, they will break them down and be upon us."

Matthew ducked behind a sofa as two men entered the room. Trying his best to remain hidden, Matthew peered cautiously around the end of the sofa. One of the men was Nicolaas van der Leyden. He was elegantly dressed in a pale green jacket. The other man, François, was evidently his servant. Matthew watched as François removed the portrait of Nicolaas van der Leyden from the wall. Van der Leyden walked to the window, looking down at the mob.

"Curse them!" he roared, shaking his fist at the angry crowd below. "Curse them all! I was so close."

"My lord, we must hurry," urged François.

"I will succeed!" thundered van der Leyden, turning away from the window. "What's this?"

Matthew had been trying to keep as still as possible, but van der Leyden had spotted him. The alchemist kicked the sofa aside with a shiny, buckled shoe, barely giving Matthew time to conceal the spell book beneath one of the nearby crates. Then van der Leyden grabbed Matthew by the collar, dragging him brutally along the floor.

"A beggar!" barked van der Leyden. "Here to see what you can steal, are you? Let's see what those riff-raff down there think when I throw you out of the window!"

Matthew tried to get away, but van der Leyden tightened his hold. He pulled his jacket aside, uncovering a pistol stuck in his belt. On the middle finger of his left hand, Matthew noticed the gold ring with the emerald stone.

"I've seen you before," van der Leyden said. "Are you a child of one of the servants? That maid, perhaps?"

Just then a tremendous crash came from the courtyard below.

"My lord!" yelled François. "The gates! We must leave. At once!"

"Curse them!" roared van der Leyden, dropping Matthew to the floor with a thump. François picked up the alchemist's portrait, while van der Leyden grabbed a small chest beside the sofa.

"Wait!" exclaimed van der Leyden. "What about the other painting?"

"I will return for it as soon as you are safely in the carriage," replied François.

Then the two men ran swiftly out of the room.

Matthew got to his feet, fetching the spell book from beneath the crate, and surveyed the chaotic scene below. The courtyard was now filled with the rampaging mob. A soldier in a dark blue uniform, complete with a red sash, forced his horse through the crowd and headed for the house. The soldier took off his hat and waved it in the air to encourage the mob.

Several burning torches shattered the upstairs windows, and the drapes burst into flames. Matthew heard the sound of breaking glass and the heavy thud of boots on the stairs.

I have to get out of here, he thought. *Please let Sally be somewhere else!*

As smoke began to fill the room, Matthew leaped once more into the painting.

CHAPTER FOURTEEN

TERROR IN TENNESSEE

Matthew fell awkwardly out of the portrait onto a thick fur rug, complete with a bear's head at one end. Looking up, he saw Peter Glimmer's picture mounted on the wall above a different fireplace. On a wall to Matthew's left hung the painting of Nicolaas van der Leyden.

Two tall wooden cabinets with etched glass doors stood against the opposite wall. Next to the cabinets, a pair of silver candlesticks sat atop a grand piano. Matthew jumped back when he saw that the drapes were in flames, and the fire was spreading. He had to find out quickly if Sally was here. Still holding the spell book, he sped out of the room, and found himself at the top of what had once been a magnificent winding staircase. Parts of the railings were blasted away, and the walls of the house had smoking holes in them.

Taking care as he went downstairs, Matthew emerged on the front veranda. Blue-uniformed soldiers on horseback galloped around the house, repeatedly firing shots. A bullet whistled past Matthew's ear, and he was suddenly aware of a man in a grey uniform crouching beside him. The man raised himself to return fire and howled in triumph as he hit one of the riders. The soldier fell from his saddle, and was dragged along by his bolting horse.

"Where did you come from, boy?" the man in the grey uniform demanded, barely glancing over his shoulder. It was Nicolaas van der Leyden!

Now clean-shaven, van der Leyden wore his hair long, as he had in 1666, but it was more unkempt. His grey uniform identified him as an officer in the Confederate Army. This was the same house Peter had shown them earlier in the frame. It was the American Civil War!

Surely he'll recognize me, thought Matthew. He then realised there was nowhere to conceal the spell book he was carrying.

Bullets whistled by them. Van der Leyden frantically returned fire, picking up one rifle after another from the collection lying beside him on the porch. In the woods opposite the house, Matthew saw a Union officer steady his horse. Matthew could also make out several soldiers rolling a cannon behind the trees.

Van der Leyden finally caught sight of the spell book in Matthew's hand, and unsheathed his sword, drawing back the blade to slash at Matthew. Just at that moment, a cannon boomed, and its shell screamed through the air, shattering the outer wall of the house. Van der Leyden staggered backwards, giving Matthew precious seconds to flee again.

The whole house was now aflame. Covering his head with his arms, Matthew raced through a wall of fire to the staircase. The first step gave way, as he scrambled up the stairs two at a time. The moment he reached the top, the entire staircase collapsed behind him. Matthew stumbled into the room where Peter's self-portrait still hung above the fireplace. He boosted himself up onto the mantelpiece, and made his escape into the canvas.

CHAPTER FIFTEEN

RUSSIAN ROULETTE

Matthew landed in a large open courtyard. The first thing he noticed was how very cold the air was. He crawled in between the picture of Peter Glimmer and at least ten other large paintings. There was deep snow on the ground and it was snowing heavily. Groups of men in heavy overcoats and fur hats, with rifles slung over their shoulders, huddled around fires to keep warm.

Soldiers, Matthew thought to himself.

At the far end of the courtyard, he could see a magnificent building. It had hundreds of windows, many of which had been smashed. The walls of the building had huge holes in them, and piles of rubble lay on the ground. More soldiers were carrying crates and rolled up carpets or tapestries down the front steps, piling them in heaps in the courtyard. Others loaded items onto carts, which were then slowly driven away.

Matthew heard voices approaching. The soldiers were starting to remove the paintings he was hidden behind! With nowhere to go, Matthew clasped the spell book to his chest and held his breath. As the canvas in front of him was lifted away, the two soldiers loading the artwork stumbled backwards in surprise. Matthew bolted across the courtyard.

"Stop!" one of the soldiers shouted after him.

Matthew looked back and saw the soldier raise his rifle to fire. Matthew dodged back and forth, expecting any second to be shot in the back. Two bullets hit the wall on either side of him, as he lunged through an open window and tumbled into a pile of hay.

He crouched down, turned, and saw through the window that the soldier had lowered his rifle. His colleagues were all laughing, slapping him on the back. Matthew watched as the portrait of Peter Glimmer was loaded onto a small horse-drawn cart with many other paintings and covered over by a blanket.

In the distance, a solitary bell tolled. The sound came from a tall, whitewashed church, topped with three gold domes. The rattle of gunfire echoed in the chilly air and red flags fluttered in the wind.

It must be St. Petersburg, during the Russian Revolution! Matthew thought.

He felt a shuffling in the hay to his left. Then he saw Sally, looking dishevelled.

"Sally!" he cried in relief.

"Matthew?" asked Sally, squinting. "Is it really you?"

"Yes," said Matthew, giving her a hug. "Have you been here long?"

"No," said Sally, brushing some of the hay from her hair. "I fell out of the canvas, just as those soldiers were carrying the portrait out to one of those piles in the courtyard. They never noticed me."

"Well, at least you're not hurt," said Matthew.

"We're not safe here, are we?" asked Sally.

"No," answered Matthew anxiously. "We have to look for a way to get back to Peter's portrait."

"But it's already gone," said Sally. She pointed into the courtyard to where the pile of valuables used to be.

"Let's try to get into one of those carts. All this stuff's probably going to the same place."

"But how do we get across the courtyard?" Sally asked. "All those soldiers…"

"Quiet!" said Matthew. "Someone's coming."

They crept out of sight as two men came into the barn and began to brush aside the hay covering a large black car.

"But, Your Excellency, this is suicide. We will never get past the guards."

"We must try, Viktor. Without that portrait, I may as well be dead."

One of the men was Nicolaas van der Leyden.

"Isn't that...?" Sally whispered.

"Shhh!" hissed Matthew.

"I was so close," growled van der Leyden as he loaded several boxes onto the car's back seat. "Damn those peasants! Are these all the notebooks, Viktor?"

"Yes, Your Excellency."

Viktor began turning a crank on the front of the car. While van der Leyden settled into the passenger seat, the engine sputtered noisily to life. When the car slowly rolled by them, Matthew spotted a wide shelf on the back of the car where the trunk should have been.

"That's how we get across the courtyard," Matthew whispered. "Come on."

Still holding the spell book, Matthew climbed onto the shelf and helped Sally up. The car began to pick up speed and, with a roar, smashed through the stable doors. Van der Leyden aimed a pistol out the side window, and two shots rang out in quick succession. As they burst free of the courtyard, the car was strafed with bullets. Matthew and Sally ducked and clung to each other, then fought to keep their balance while the car wound through the streets of St. Petersburg.

A short while later, the car rolled to a stop in front of a warehouse on the waterfront. Matthew and Sally slipped down and tucked themselves behind a stack of barrels.

The two men stepped cautiously out of the bullet-ridden car.

"Take care, Viktor," advised van der Leyden, as he tossed his servant a pistol. "The guards inside will be well armed. Shoot to kill."

Van der Leyden and Viktor approached the warehouse entrance, then disappeared into the building.

"So what now?" whispered Sally.

"We've got to find Peter's portrait. Follow me," said Matthew, creeping along the outside wall.

Through a broken window, Matthew and Sally saw that the warehouse was crammed with paintings, statues and sculptures. Against the walls, countless rolled up carpets and tapestries were stacked beside elegant-looking tables, chairs, and chests.

Van der Leyden was standing with his back to them, examining his portrait. Matthew noticed a soldier, wearing a fur hat, huddled in the darkness behind a crate. The soldier raised his rifle, and a shot rang out. Viktor fell to the ground. Two more shots exploded. The soldier keeled over and there was silence. Matthew and Sally watched as Nicolaas van der Leyden staggered and fell to the floor, dropping his gun. They could see blood streaming from a wound above his left eyebrow. He lay still.

"Look!" exclaimed Sally. "It's Peter's portrait!"

Sure enough, Peter's face was unmistakable, staring out from the familiar frame. The painting was leaning against a crate near van der Leyden's motionless form. Tucking the spell book under his arm, Matthew climbed over the windowsill. Sally followed carefully, navigating the broken glass.

"Do you think he's dead?" Sally asked, warily, staring down at van der Leyden on the bloodstained floor.

"He can't be. He's still alive back in our own time as Albert Runsiman. Runsiman has a scar above his left eye. Now we know how he got it."

"We'd better escape through the time portal before he recovers," said Sally.

"Hold onto me," Matthew told Sally, as he placed one hand on the canvas.

Holding the spell book with his other hand, Matthew stepped into the canvas. But before he could enter the time portal, he felt Sally being jerked backwards.

"Matthew!" she screamed.

Matthew turned around to see that Nicolaas van der Leyden had grabbed his sister by the ankle.

"I know you!" van der Leyden bellowed at Matthew. His face and hair were now covered in blood. "I do know you! You're that boy! It's impossible! And you! You're that girl from the attic!"

Still lying on the floor, van der Leyden reached for his gun. At the same time, Matthew toppled a pile of paintings, burying the alchemist under them. While van der Leyden struggled to get free, Matthew quickly jumped into Peter's portrait with Sally holding firmly onto his waist.

CHAPTER SIXTEEN

THE NEW APPRENTICE

Matthew and Sally were back inside Peter's portrait, and Peter himself was there to greet them.

"What happened?" said Matthew, handing Peter the spell book.

"The time stream was altered," said Peter. "I should never have sent you back. But thank God you are safe."

"Only just," said Matthew. "We could have been killed! In fact we almost were. More than once."

"Please forgive my inexperience," begged Peter. "The presence of you and Sally in the past led to complications I could not anticipate."

"But now everything's all right?" Sally queried.

"The time stream is now restored," said Peter. "But the threat from my uncle remains."

"When we left him in Russia," said Sally, "he was badly injured. How did he survive?"

"I am afraid that he did survive," said Peter. "Everything is nearly the same as before you travelled back to 1666. There are two important differences. The first is that I have the spell book, thanks to you and Sally. The second difference is that last night, in your time period, Runsiman finished restoring the face in his portrait, using the magic paint. The restoration is now complete, and my uncle is now about to enter the portrait and achieve immortality. If he does so, his full powers will be restored, and he will be able to take over the world. The vision of the future that I showed you will become a reality."

"How can we stop him?" asked Matthew, deeply worried.

"You must prevent my uncle from entering his restored portrait, until I find the spell that will free me from my entrapment here," Peter answered. "Once I free myself, I will come to your assistance in your own time."

"Why don't you just learn the time travel spell and go straight back in time to help your father?" asked Matthew.

"It is essential that we first stop my uncle from entering the portrait," Peter gravely explained as he flipped through the spell book. "There is too much at stake. We cannot take any chances. There is no way to know if I will succeed in my mission to save my father's life and stop my uncle before he begins his evil work."

"I see," said Matthew. "You want to stop your uncle in my time, before you travel back to the time before your father was murdered."

Peter nodded. "If we are able to succeed in your time, then I will use the time travel spell to take a one way trip into the past to save my father, and bring my uncle to justice. It will be up to you, Matthew, to delay Runsiman from entering his portrait until I can come to your aid."

"Up to me!" exclaimed Matthew.

"Yes. You. But first, Sally, you must get to safety. Your brother will follow shortly."

"But I want to..." Sally began to protest.

"I can't protect you if you stay, Sally. You must trust me, and go back now," said Peter.

The frame once again showed the Portrait Gallery. Reluctantly, Sally stepped into it, back to her own time.

"It's up to you now, Matthew," said Peter.

"Do you want me to destroy your uncle's portrait?" Matthew asked.

"No. Your task will not be so simple, I am afraid. You will not be able to destroy the painting. My uncle has protected it with a powerful spell," answered Peter. "It has been partly damaged many times over the centuries, but it is virtually indestructible. You may have to engage my uncle in combat, and I will give you the powers you will need to stave him off until I can join you. His own powers have been considerably weakened over the years, but he is still a formidable opponent."

Peter then placed his hand on Matthew's shoulder and Mathew felt a surge of energy rush through his body.

"I am transferring some of my own powers to you," said Peter. "They will enable you to hold off Runsiman, until I find the correct spell to release me. Only then will I be able to help you."

"But, what if you don't find a way to break out of your portrait prison?" a worried Matthew asked.

Peter retreated into the shadows of the room. "You have the power now," Matthew heard him say. "Gather up your courage. You must succeed!"

Then Matthew was back in the gallery.

But he wasn't alone! Albert Runsiman stood directly across from him.

"You're that same boy!" he said, his cold grey eyes staring at Matthew. "When I saw you in the car with Tess, I decided to stop you once and for all. I saw you enter the painting just now. You have been a thorn in my flesh for the last time! After I get rid of you, I'll deal with Tess and that girl from the attic!"

Runsiman glared at Tess and Sally across the room.

"You had better say your prayers quickly," he said with a dark smile.

"I'm sorry I doubted you, Matthew," Tess apologized. "Sally told me everything."

"I see that my secret is out. Yes, I am Nicolaas van der Leyden," he said. "But it no longer matters if anyone knows."

"Get down!" yelled Tess.

She pushed Matthew and Sally to the floor, as a ball of white flame roared towards them. Tess received the full force of van der Leyden's attack, and was blasted across the gallery.

"Tess!" screamed Matthew.

"My nephew must still be alive. He is more clever than I ever could have thought possible," said van der

113

Leyden, casually stepping over Tess's body. Matthew dodged as another flame shot out from van der Leyden's hand, striking Peter Glimmer's portrait.

"I have spent centuries trying to discover Johan Glimmer's formula," sneered van der Leyden. "Do you really think you can defeat me at my moment of triumph, boy?"

You have the power now, Matthew heard Peter's voice whisper.

Looking at his hand, Matthew saw a flame begin to flicker at the tips of his fingers. Then, while pointing his arm at van der Leyden, he concentrated. He was astounded to see a white-hot flame leap from his own hand directly at van der Leyden. The alchemist gaped in disbelief, as he was thrown against the wall.

"Get out of the museum!" Matthew ordered Sally. "There's no telling how long he'll be out."

"But what about you? What about Tess?" Sally protested.

"You'll be safer on your own," said Matthew. "Just go!"

Matthew watched her run out of the Portrait Gallery, and disappear down the corridor that led to the main exit. Then he ran into the Sculpture Gallery.

His heart skipped a beat when he turned to see van der Leyden following him.

"How do you expect to win?" shouted van der Leyden, his hand fully ablaze.

As Matthew turned around and ran, a white flame knocked him off his feet. He crawled behind a statue, but it was blasted into pieces. Van der Leyden prepared to fire again, but Matthew managed to race from the room.

He found himself near the mosaic in the centre of the museum. Corridors and exits led in every direction.

"Run all you like," screeched van der Leyden behind him, "but you'll never escape!"

Matthew whirled around to face him. The flame from van der Leyden's hand was now white hot. Matthew leaped aside, as a stream of fire struck the dragon's head on the Viking ship, which burst into flames. He watched in horror as the burning longboat was lifted up, suspended above him in mid-air.

"Don't expect any help," van der Leyden said, with a cruel laugh. "There will be no alarms. The museum guards don't realise this is happening. I have a spell for everything!"

Then the longship dropped like a stone. Matthew just managed to get out of the way. He then used his new powers to make a heavy carving fly off the wall. It knocked van der Leyden to the ground.

I have to destroy the alchemist's portrait! Matthew thought desperately.

CHAPTER SEVENTEEN

THE ALCHEMIST'S POWER

Despite what Peter had said about van der Leyden's portrait being indestructible, Matthew couldn't see what else he could do but attempt to destroy the painting.

The Restoration Room hadn't changed, except for the portrait of Nicolaas van der Leyden, which was now finished. The stern figure looked exactly as he had when Matthew encountered him in 1666. He was even wearing the gold ring with the green gemstone. The only difference between van der Leyden and Runsiman was the scar on Runsiman's forehead.

Matthew saw what he assumed was the magic paint on a side table. *Portrait first, paint later,* he decided. He concentrated. When he saw flames flickering out of his fingertips, he took aim at the canvas.

I hope this works, he prayed.

Before he could fire, the door of the Restoration Room was blown apart, and Nicolaas van der Leyden blasted Matthew right through the wall into the Egyptian Room. The enormous mummy case fell forward and missed him by inches.

"You've got more lives than a cat!" van der Leyden shouted, as he stood in the gaping hole, silhouetted against the fire spreading rapidly through the Restoration Room behind him. "But your lives are about to run out!"

Matthew jumped to one side as more flames shot toward him, shattering the surrounding cases and littering the floor with broken glass. One of the mummies tumbled out, its leathery skin brushing Matthew's arm as it fell. Within seconds, the Egyptian Room was in flames.

By now, Matthew was exhausted.

"You're finished, boy!" van der Leyden roared, rushing at him.

Just as the alchemist moved in for the kill, a powerful blow rocked him.

"Peter!" said Matthew. "Thank goodness you finally got out!"

"Stay down," ordered Peter, placing a reassuring hand on Matthew's shoulder.

"Peter!" exclaimed a breathless van der Leyden, looking dazed.

"Prepare to die, Uncle," said Peter. "I am here to avenge my father's death!"

"You can never defeat me," said van der Leyden. "You're no more than an apprentice! I'll kill you just like I killed your father!"

Then Matthew saw statue after statue advancing upon them.

"Quickly, Matthew!" ordered Peter. "Help me destroy them!"

Peter and Matthew fired at the moving statues, blasting them to pieces one by one. The statue with four arms was more difficult to stop. It moved with lightning speed, scooping up shards of glass and flinging them at Matthew and Peter in a ferocious volley. Matthew finally scored a direct hit, shattering it into a thousand pieces.

"It's not over yet!" yelled van der Leyden.

Eight suits of armour now advanced towards the boys, all heavily armed with axes, swords and spears.

One after another, the suits of armour threw their weapons, while Peter struggled in vain to conjure up a shield to defend Matthew and himself. It took repeated blasts to destroy the attackers, but one suit of armour got through. It carried a broadsword five feet long and caught Peter on the side of his head. He staggered backwards and slumped to the floor.

"Now I have you!" said Nicolaas van der Leyden. Visibly weakened, he lurched through the rising flames. "Peter can't help you now."

Matthew heard what sounded like thunder, coming closer and closer. Then it was silent, and Matthew realised that it wasn't thunder at all. In the doorway leading out into the corridor, through the flames, he could make out the armoured horse. The knight on its back lowered his lance. The thundering returned as the ghostly hooves pawed the Egyptian Room floor and the knight prepared to charge. Matthew concentrated as hard as he could, but the flame refused to ignite at his fingertips. His powers had gone!

"Peter!" he shouted. "Peter! Wake up!"

But no matter how much Matthew shook him, Peter didn't respond. Van der Leyden cackled wildly, his laughter becoming a maniacal shriek as the horse and knight leaped through the flames and raced towards

Matthew. Matthew closed his eyes tightly, but a terrific flash of light made him open them again. In front of him, the horse and knight were a pile of twisted metal. The lance lay where it had fallen, beside his feet.

Matthew watched the alchemist stumble through the flames towards the hole in the wall and disappear into the Restoration Room.

"Quickly! We must catch him," gulped Peter, struggling to get up. His hair was thickly matted with blood. "We must stop him before he has a chance to enter the painting!"

They clambered through the shattered wall and over the mound of rubble, into what was left of the Restoration Room. Once there, Matthew watched in horror, as van der Leyden began to enter his portrait.

"Soon, my powers will be fully restored," said van der Leyden, as he melted into the canvas. "And make no mistake, you shall both perish!"

"No, Uncle," said Peter, leaning on Matthew for support. "It is you who shall perish!"

Peter raised his right hand and Matthew watched as a brilliant green glow surrounded Peter's outstretched fingers. The glow shot out of the centre of his palm at van der Leyden's portrait.

"No! Not when I'm this close!" van der Leyden wailed. He was now completely at one with the canvas.

A green cloud enveloped the painting for an instant, followed by van der Leyden's shrill scream. When the cloud lifted, the face in the painting now had a scar above its left eye.

Van der Leyden's spell has been broken, Matthew thought.

The museum alarms began to blare loudly.

"What did you do?" Matthew shouted over the noise.

"I trapped van der Leyden in his own portrait using a variation of the spell that he used on me in 1666," Peter replied.

"But he had the magic paint. He'll be immortal!" protested Matthew.

"No, Matthew," said Peter, at the top of his voice. "The portrait had to be the *exact* image in order to work properly. The face in the painting was the way it looked *when my father painted him.* Van der Leyden had no scar back then. It was a small detail, but a detail that cost him his life. I realised his mistake, when I saw him standing in front of the finished portrait."

"So he's trapped inside his own portrait now, in the same way that you were trapped in yours!"

"Yes. But I must now get back to the time portal. Thank you, Matthew," said Peter, as he turned to leave the Restoration Room.

"Sally!" exclaimed Matthew, catching sight of his sister and Tess in the shattered doorway. "And Tess! Are you okay?"

There was a deep gash on Tess's left cheek, and her right arm had severe burns. She had the beginnings of a black eye.

"Peter Glimmer!" she gasped.

"Look out!" shouted Matthew, ducking as van der Leyden's arm suddenly stretched out from the canvas.

Matthew grabbed Tess and Sally and pulled them to the floor with him as a flame shot across the room, igniting the pictures. Soon, the entire Restoration Room was on fire.

"I must move quickly!" said Peter. "To the Portrait Gallery!"

"You two have to get out of here," Matthew yelled, pushing them towards the door.

"But the paintings!" said Tess, desperately trying to gather up her materials from among the overturned tables. "All my work!"

"There's no time for that!" yelled Matthew. "Run!"

As Matthew followed Peter through the corridors to the Portrait Gallery, he could hear sirens in the street.

It won't be long before the fire-fighters and the police show up, Matthew thought. *I'll have a lot of explaining to do, especially if I'm with a kid in strange clothes who claims to be from 1666!*

"It should still work," said Peter as they came to a halt in front of his portrait.

The portrait and the carved frame hadn't been damaged at all by van der Leyden's attack.

"I saw your uncle blast the painting with fire," said Matthew.

"The civilisation that created the carvings possessed powers we can only guess at, Matthew," said Peter. "The frame protects both the painting and the time portal."

Peter turned to face Matthew. "The spell that will take me back in time is a one-way journey. I must use it wisely, for afterwards the portal will no longer function. I intend to change history," said Peter, boldly, "to be doubly certain van der Leyden is destroyed."

"But you imprisoned him in his portrait, didn't you?" said Matthew.

"I know," said Peter, "but my uncle was a powerful magician. I have to make sure he never threatens the world again. Back in my time, there is enough evidence from van der Leyden's medical experiments and spell book to convict him as a purveyor of black magic. I plan to go back far enough in time to save my father's life. I will even try to prevent my mother's premature death."

Smoke began to enter the Portrait Gallery from the adjoining corridor. The fire was spreading out of control.

"But if your plan works," said Matthew, frowning, "wouldn't that mean you were never imprisoned in the portrait and none of this ever happened?"

"Yes, I believe that will be the case. Your memory of recent events, and the memories of your sister and friends, will be erased. Take this."

"What is it?" Matthew asked as Peter pressed something into his hand.

"The emerald from my uncle's ring," said Peter. "It fell out when he made his last attack. Take it."

Mathew held the gemstone in his palm, turning it over with his fingers.

"And now, farewell. I must go," declared Peter.

Then Peter Glimmer disappeared into the canvas.

Matthew stood on the sidewalk, watching the fire-fighters struggle to bring the blaze under control. He wondered if he still had any of the powers he'd been given, but his fingers stubbornly refused to burst into flame. Sally, meanwhile, sat in the back of an ambulance, sipping a hot drink.

"Will she be okay?" Matthew asked the paramedics as they carried Tess into another ambulance waiting nearby.

"Sure," said the medic, closing the ambulance doors. "She should be fine in a couple of days."

Matthew saw a mop of red hair bobbing up and down through the crowd gathered behind the yellow police tape. "Matthew!" shouted Alex. Alex ducked under the tape and headed towards him. "Hey man! I'm so glad you're okay. I saw a news clip of the fire on television and knew it was you..."

"Excuse me."

Matthew turned around to face a police sergeant towering over him. He looked up at him, then over at Sally in the ambulance. Matthew gave the officer a smile, which he didn't return.

"We'd like to ask you and your sister a few questions," he said gruffly.

EPILOGUE

"It's an interesting piece, isn't it?"

Matthew was in a daze, but turned away from the portrait in front of him to see a tall, slim, smartly dressed young woman beside him. Her hair was very short, much shorter than his own, and her wrists were covered with more bracelets than he could count. The nametag on her lapel read Tess Philips, Restoration Manager. *Matthew felt he knew her, but couldn't remember why.*

"Yes, it is," said Matthew.

The man in the portrait appeared to be in his mid-forties, with jet-black hair and a wide-brimmed black hat. His beard was flecked with grey, and a contented smile was evident beneath his thick moustache. Beside him was a beautiful woman, whose sandy hair tumbled over a wide, lace collar. A boy, with the same sandy hair, sat between them at the forefront of the painting, beaming out at Matthew.

"Who were they?" Matthew asked.

"This is a portrait by Johan Glimmer, of himself, his wife Anna and son Peter," said Tess. "Glimmer was a well-known artist in seventeenth-century Amsterdam. He was also an alchemist, and a medical pioneer. His

son grew up to follow in his father's footsteps. Peter Glimmer became one of that century's most renowned scientists."

"Really?" said Matthew, intrigued.

"But," Tess went on, "Anna Glimmer had a brother named Nicolaas van der Leyden. He was an alchemist too, but was rumoured to be involved with witchcraft."

"Witchcraft?" said Matthew.

"Yes," said Tess. "He was tried in court for witchcraft and executed."

"Really?" asked Matthew. "That's amazing!"

"Yes," said Tess. "There was a book of black magic spells found in his house, along with a journal detailing all his illegal medical work. Nicolaas van der Leyden was brought to trial and executed in 1666."

"Hey, Matthew," called a voice, right beside him. It was his friend, Alex. "Are you coming or not? Goring said we can all go to the cafeteria for lunch."

"Huh?" murmured Matthew.

"Come on," said Alex, as he hurried to rejoin the rest of the school group.

"I have to go," Matthew told Tess. "Thanks."

"You're welcome," said Tess with a smile.

Johan and Peter Glimmer? Van der Leyden? Why do I know those names and faces? *thought Matthew, as he hurried to catch up with Alex.*

He couldn't recall. Perhaps he'd read something in the museum guidebook. Confusing images flashed across Matthew's mind while he accompanied his classmates to the cafeteria. It was like struggling to recall the details of a dream.

As Matthew stuck his hand in his pocket to pay his cafeteria bill, he felt something odd. When he pulled his hand out, a large emerald lay in his palm, glinting in the light. His tray clattered to the floor. Staring at the green gemstone in his hand, Matthew remembered everything.